I0532566

LOVE

REDEEMED

Praise for Tich Brewster's
Love Redeemed

"Great story of love lost and found again and the struggles they go through to get to know each other again."

~Jennifer Wedmore, 2 Bibliophiles Guide

"I just LOVED these characters! You can't help but feel for them and you'll find yourself rooting for them all the way through the book. They belong together. This book totally rocked! I highly recommend you read this one!

~Brenda Romine, Loves All Things Books

"Tich Brewster stole my heart with this heartwarming love story. Not only did she nail each character to the tee she told their story like only an experienced author could do."

~Dawn Cripps, I Love Books

"This book also has some great twists and turns and you will truly be surprised. Fabulous job. Can't wait for another book Tich."

~Risha Crider, Reviewer

LOVE

REDEEMED

TICH BREWSTER

This is a work of fiction. All names, characters, places, and events are the work of the author's imagination. Any resemblance to real person, places, or events is coincidental.

Pennedit Publishing

Tulsa, OK

Love Redeemed
ISBN-10: 0615881777
ISBN-13: 978-0615881775
Published by Pennedit 2013
penneditpublishing.com

All rights reserved. No part of this book may be reproduced or transmitted in any form or by any means, electronic or mechanical, including photocopying, recording, without permission in writing from the author.
Scanning, uploading, and distribution of this book via the Internet or by any other means without permission are illegal and punishable by law.

Copyright 2013 © Leticha Brewster
Cover Art: Sprinkles On Top Studios

sprinklesontopstudios.com
Editing: Twilight Hours Editing
twilighthoursedits.blogspot.com
Proofreading/Editing: Jessica's Author/Book
Promoting and Proofreading Services
facebook.com/JessiPromotions

Acknowledgements

First I have to give thanks to my Lord and Savior Jesus Christ. Without Him I am nothing but it is because of Him that I am a conqueror. I can do all things through Christ who gives me strength (Philippians 4:13)

I have several people that deserve a huge thank you for supporting me and encouraging me along the way. My husband is my biggest supporter and the love of my life. I am eternally grateful that God brought us together. A thank you goes out to my Momma, Daddy and Mom Rhonda, as well as my Grandma and all my children. Teresa Fuentez, I owe you a humongous thank you for pushing me to publish. If it hadn't been for you, I would still be writing in my notebooks for my own entertainment.

And of course Chumeica Paden, girl you have been the best cheerleader a girl could have.

Special Thanks

There are several people that deserve a special thank you!

A thank you goes out to Jessica Sawa for choosing Ryder's name. To the ones that wrote a song for Ryder, thank you so much. Andrea L. Staum wrote Temptation, Ti Colluney wrote Come Back, and Tom Brewster wrote Our Love is like Fire. Now, for all of my beta readers: Brenda Romine, Jennifer Wedmore, Shalisha Cooper, Tonya Rupell, and Sheri Spell, a huge thank you goes out to you for your feedback and support.   XOXOXO

Chapter One

Cassie Strong stood in front of her bedroom mirror trying to decide which outfit looked best on her, the black and aqua lace dress or the red flare dress. Tonight was her best friend's birthday. She had been friends with Allie Walsh since middle school.

Tonight she wanted to look great for her friend's special day. In celebration of Allie's birthday Cassie and Jared Sullivan, Allie's boyfriend, were taking Allie to the local club.

She held the red dress up to her body. It was a little more casual with a v-neckline and fitted bodice. She tossed it back onto the bed and held up the lace dress. This one was quite a bit shorter, mid-thigh. It also had a sweetheart neckline that showed a small amount of cleavage.

Tonight Cassie was going to relax and enjoy life, live a little on the wild side. She had every intention on dancing, having a drink, and possibly flirting with a guy or two. Something she hadn't done too much of since high school.

The lace dress would be perfect for such an occasion. She slipped it on and twirled a few times, admiring the way it clung to her small frame. Hopefully she could find those sparkly black pumps to complete her look.

Knock...knock. Allie was here early. They weren't supposed to leave for another hour. "Just a minute," she yelled as she raced down the hallway to the front door.

As she opened the door she was taken aback by the man greeting her with a smile. She was expecting Allie not Jared. Jared had his raven black hair combed over one eye. She would never understand why he did that. If she wore her hair over her eyes she'd end up with a killer headache before her day fully began.

"Jared, come in." She stepped aside to let him in. "I was expecting Allie."

"She had a hair appointment." He sat down on her couch, resting his right foot on his left knee. "So Ryder is..."

She cut him off before he could say another word. "You are not allowed to say that name and you know it."

"Yes, but I thought…"

Again, she cut him off. "You thought wrong. I know he's your best friend and you love him but his name is off limits, especially in my home."

"Suite yourself," he smirked. He picked up the novel on her end table and examined the cover. "You read trashy novels?"

She snatched the paperback out of his hand. "It's not trashy, it's romance. There's a big difference." He chuckled at her. He actually chuckled at her, the nerve of that man. How dare he make fun of her and her choice of books? She hit him upside the head with her beloved book.

"Fine, it's not trashy." He threw his hands up in surrender. "Now go get ready, we have to pick up Allie." When she glanced down at her dress with a questioning look he continued, "You need shoes if you're going with me."

"Oh, I was about to say." She went in search of the sparkly pumps that she loved so much. They were in the bottom of her closet, buried under her massive shoe collection. She definitely needed to think about adding some shelving in her room just for her shoes.

She added some curl to the ends of her hair and some color to her lips before joining Jared in the other room. He was stretched out on the sofa, one hand behind his head, and yet another book in his hand.

When Cassie noticed the book he was reading she gasped and ran toward him, jerking the paperback out of his grasp. "You can't read that." She hid the book behind her back.

He smiled a knowing smile. She was pretty sure by that look that he already knew the contents of the book she held. If only a giant hole would form under her and swallow her whole. She tossed the book back on the bookshelf, grabbed her purse, and headed for the door.

Allie was waiting for them when they arrived at the spa to pick her up. Her hair was pulled back and a few blonde locks fell loosely around her face. Jared greeted his girlfriend with a kiss and then they were off to the club.

The ride there was fairly short. The spa was just around the corner from Club Jamz. The three of them had arrived early enough to miss the heavy crowd at the door. ID's were checked and the trio made their way to the bar.

The music pulsated through the building, vibrating the walls and floor. Cassie sat on a bar stool, tapping her fingers in time with the music. The one thing she enjoyed about this club was the live bands, not that she came here that often.

Jared jerked his thumb behind him. "You girls want to dance with me?"

Allie pulled Cassie off of the stool she had just sat on. "Let's go have some fun," she shouted above the noise.

Cassie didn't have to be asked twice. It had been a year since she had gone out and enjoyed herself for the night. She followed her friends out to the dance floor. Jared pulled Allie flush against his left hip and tugged Cassie towards his right hip.

It took her a minute to flow into a rhythm. She wasn't used to dancing in a trio. Heck, she wasn't used to dancing with a partner, period. By the third song she had it mastered.

There was a soft tap on her shoulder. A deep voice spoke next to her ear. "Care to dance with me?"

A smile spread on her face when he tipped his cowboy hat with a wink. "Sure." She broke free of her friends and joined hands with her new dance partner.

"I'm William." He placed his hands on her waist.

"Cassie." They moved their bodies back and forth. The music had changed over from live to CD while the bands switched up on stage. They danced a total of a song and a half when the next band took the stage.

The club owner announced the upcoming band but she was too busy laughing to hear the name. Once again, the place vibrated with thumping music. She froze as her mind registered what she was hearing. She knew that song, she had played it every day when she was younger. She stopped dancing, slowly turning to face the stage.

His voice boomed over the speakers, that deep throaty voice that she knew all too well. "Panic hits but it's too late. Too late to say what you needed to hear. You needed to hear just how much I need you. And now you took the better part of me."

Pushing through the crowd was tough but she had to see for herself. When she had a clear view of the stage she lifted her eyes to meet the lead singer. Ryder.

As if sensing her eyes on him, his eyes traveled over the sea of faces until they landed on her. He still looked the same as he did the last time she saw him eight years ago, his messy dark brown hair, faded blue jeans, and that ugly black fingerless glove on his right hand. She couldn't believe that he still wore that thing.

In that one moment, with just one look into his eyes, all those feelings that she had finally buried deep within, resurfaced. The love they once shared and the heartache she suffered when he walked away. She couldn't do this, couldn't be in the same room with him. If she didn't get out of there and away from him then that wall she worked so hard to build around her heart would crumble to the ground.

Chapter Two

Cassie stormed through the crowd of dancing people but was halted by a viselike grip on her arm, above the elbow. "Come on, Cass. It's my birthday, you can't leave," Allie pleaded.

Jared looked up at the stage then back at her. "Don't go. Forget everything and enjoy yourself. And like she said," he pointed at his girlfriend. "It is her birthday. Don't skip out on her because of that boneheaded jerk on stage."

Cassie warred with the idea of staying for her friend and doing the smart thing, leaving before her heart shattered. Again. She looked back at the stage. Ryder was no longer looking in her direction. Maybe she could get through the night without having to speak to him. "Fine, I'll stay."

She had to admit, Ryder looked pretty darn good on stage. Music was who he was, she always knew that. She should have seen that day coming long before it ever arrived. He thrived on the bass pounding through the floor and vibrating up his body. The screaming fans gave him a high he could never get enough of.

Jared held his hands up in surrender. "Hey, I tried to tell you. You're the one that told me to never speak of him."

She did, didn't she? Well crap. That's what she gets for tuning everything Ryder out. She thought a little longer and her love for her friend won over. "I'm fine. I'm a big girl." As long as she kept her eyes off of the stage, she could get through this evening in one piece.

She ordered an Ice Bomb, drinking a little faster than normal. She ignored the stares from her friends and ordered another. At this rate she'd end up beyond drunk but at least the alcohol would numb her heart.

An hour and four Ice Bomb's later; Cassie began to feel the nasty effects of her choice in drinks, or amount of drinks. She stood on wobbly legs, took two steps back, and bumped into someone. Not just someone. Ryder.

The giggle escaped before she could stop it. "Well, if it isn't the rock star." Her speech was slurred. She had never been much of a drinker and with the amount she had just consumed, she was surprised that she was still among the living. Focusing was getting harder by the minute. Next time she drank she'd have to remember to keep it light, or not anything alcoholic. Jeez, was it getting hot in here?

Heat spread through her cheeks, tinting them a bright shade of red. She didn't need a mirror to know just how ridiculous she must look. Right now she wished she could jump into oblivion just to hide from the whole world.

Ryder crossed his arms over his chest. Did the smug jerk actually chuckle at her? She needed fresh air and she needed it now. She walked around him, or at least that was her intent. Instead, the heel of her shoe caught on something and she lost her balance.

Time seemed to slow down and her fall passed in slow motion. Had she been sober this would have gone differently but unfortunately for her, she wasn't.

Her drunkenness got the best of her and she landed hard on her backside. Where was a re-do button when you needed one? Embarrassment gnawed away at her, tears forming in her eyes. If this had happened in front of any other guy it might not bother her as much but this was Ryder.

A hand appeared in front her. Her eyes traveled the length of the arm and into the eyes of Ryder. He was not laughing at her nor did he look amused. He simply said, "Come on, Cass. I'll take you home."

Cassie glanced over at her friends. Jared nodded towards Ryder with a thumbs-up, but of course he would approve of her getting a ride home with his longtime friend. Allie smiled. "Go on Cassie. You'll be fine."

Would she? How could she possibly be fine if she left with this man? This man that took her heart, broke it into tiny pieces, and then pureed it before throwing it back in her face.

Ryder knelt down, turned her head to face him. "Let me take you home." Again, he extended his hand.

She really didn't have much of a choice. Jared and Allie had no intensions of leaving early to take her home. She accepted his hand and allowed him to pull her to her feet. He steadied her by placing his arm around her shoulders. When he did, a small piece of that wall she had built around her heart crumbled.

Chapter Three

Ryder opened every cabinet in Cassie's kitchen until he found the one housing her collection of flavored tea. He glanced back into the living room, she lay sprawled out on the sofa. If anyone ever looked green it was her. Her skin was pale, dark circles formed under her eyes.

He set a pot of water on the stove to boil then went in search of a wash rag to wet for her forehead. If this was the same girl he knew eight years ago, she had no business drinking more than one glass of any kind of alcohol. She'd always been a lightweight.

He laughed at her bathroom. Not that it was terribly decorated or messy, just the opposite. Periwinkle walls with bright white trim, stainless steel accessories, and a counter topped with several wash rags folded into little fans. He unfolded a rag and wet it with cold water.

As he approached the sofa she groaned, covering her mouth with a hand. A second later she breathed deeply in through the nose and out through the mouth. He placed the cool rag on her forehead. Her eyes shot open, glaring at him. Apparently, she thought that he had just dumped her on the sofa and left her to rot in the vomit that was sure to make an appearance.

Sitting up, she jerked the rag from his grip. He wondered why she was being so hostile. Heck, before he started touring they were dating, they were in love. She had always proclaimed that he was the only one that would hold the key to her heart, so what on earth was this attitude about? When his last tour ended he was thrilled to have this opportunity to come back home, to see his friends and family, to spend some time with Cassie.

"I can take care of myself. You're free to leave." She turned her head. "Again," she whispered so low he almost missed it.

"I'm sure you can." He left her side to finish making the tea.

Deciding which flavor to make for her was not an easy task. There must have been twenty boxes, each a different brand and flavor. Closing his eyes, he reached into the cabinet and grabbed the first box his hand landed on, Mixed Berry.

He took the pan of boiling water to the sink to pour it into the coffee mug. Dropping the tea bag in the mug to brew, he went in search of honey.

"Honey or sugar?" She never added sugar to her tea before but he thought he'd ask in case that had changed over the years.

He heard her get up off the sofa. Her angry footsteps grew louder as she neared the kitchen. Who knew such a tiny body could stomp so loudly. "Not that you actually care, but I prefer nothing in my tea."

Setting the honey back on the counter he asked, "What's that supposed to mean?" He turned around to face her.

She crossed her arms over her chest. "I mean that you don't care, not about me or what I want."

Where had that come from? "I most certainly do care. You're my friend, one of my best friends, my former lover."

"Best friends don't leave without a word and never look back. Boyfriends, lovers, they don't just pack up and leave the one they love behind." She threw the rag at him. It failed to hit the target, instead it landed at his feet. "You can go home."

He wasn't sure why she was mad. It must be the alcohol because the Cassie he knew was the kindest, most loving girl on earth. He set her tea on the kitchen table. "Okay. Well, here's your tea."

Cassie watched Ryder walk out of her front door. He didn't try to defend himself and he didn't look back. Somehow, this felt like eight years ago. Why did he have to step foot back into this town?

As soon as the door clicked shut she stormed to the kitchen table, picked up her tea, and slammed the mug into the sink with a shout of frustration. The only mug she owned shattered in the sink, pieces flying up on the counter. The handle bounced up to smack her on the nose as if to say, you spoiled brat.

Chapter Four

Cassie woke up the next morning with the worst hangover ever. Every noise, every light, caused her head to throb to the point she thought it'd crack open. She'd be surprised if her eyes didn't pop out of her head. What had gotten into her last night? She couldn't even remember getting home. She groaned and glanced at her alarm clock.

One look at the clock and she jumped up, rushing to the shower. How could she sleep through the alarm? That thing was insanely loud.

Was it broken? That had to be it, it was the only explanation.

She took the quickest shower of her life. Her boss was going to kill her. She was two hours late for work. She didn't even bother to dry her hair, there wasn't enough time. She pulled it into a low ponytail, applied a layer of lip gloss, and walked out the door.

It took her a total of two steps to realize that she was missing something, she was empty-handed. She ran back inside to fetch her briefcase. It was essential, she couldn't work without it.

The Texas heat was a scorching 102° on this mid July morning. Thank goodness for air conditioning otherwise her thirty minute ride to work would have given her a heat stroke.

Cassie stood in front of her office building and dug in her purse for the bottle of Ibuprofen. She popped two pills, washing them down with her morning energy drink. That wasn't the best way to start her day by any means, but this was her consequence to pay for last night.

She squared her shoulders and walked into the building. Every head turned to stare. They eyed her like they knew what she had done the previous night and why she had done it. She smiled at her co-workers and continued to her small office cubicle. A note lay across her computer keyboard. **My office. NOW!**

Yikes, a note from the boss. She set her briefcase on the desk and went to the office where her boss was waiting for her.

"Close the door." Mr. Bradshaw didn't even look up at her, he just pointed to the chair directly in front of his desk. "Sit."

She sat, nervously tapping her fingers on her thigh. "You wanted to see me, Sir?"

He tapped a few more keys on his computer, sipped his coffee, and pointed a pencil in her direction. "You're late for work."

She took a deep breath. Should she explain that she went out to celebrate her friend's birthday? That it had been a late night and she had overslept? Mr. Bradshaw looked at her expectantly. No, that would sound like she was just making excuses. "I apologize, Sir. It will not happen again."

He turned back to his computer screen. "See that it doesn't. This is a business and we have deadlines to meet." With that he waved her away.

She had never felt so humiliated in her life. Since starting this job four years ago she had never been in trouble with the boss. She was the best editor that this company had, even her co-workers asked her for advice.

She went back to her desk and fired up her computer. The manuscript she had been working on was due by the end of the week and she was only halfway through it.   As soon as the document loaded she received a notification, she had an email.

She clicked on the icon, loading her email. It might be urgent.   Her clients emailed her regularly with questions or just wanting an update on their manuscript. She opened the message. **Can we talk, maybe for lunch or dinner? –R**

R? Who in the world was R? She replied, **Who is this?   –Cassie Strong, Editor of Bradshaw Publishing**

She switched back over to the manuscript, not expecting the messenger to respond for a while. Not two seconds after she had hit send another email notification popped up. **Oh, sorry. It's me, Ryder. –R**

Oh this was so not what she expected, or needed, this morning.   She was hoping that last night had just been a total nightmare.   That she hadn't made a total fool of herself in front of him. No such luck. **No. –Cassie Strong, Editor of Bradshaw Publishing**

He didn't deserve any explanations from her. She was not interested in hearing anything he had to say either. Another message popped up. **I would love the chance to catch up. –R**

Jeez, the man was infuriating. Did she use a word too complex for him? No meant that she had no desire to meet up with him. **Do you need a dictionary? –Cassie Strong, Editor of Bradshaw Publishing**

Another message came through. It was instantaneous. She doubted he had time to see her last reply. **Come on, I miss you. –R**

She rolled her eyes. *He misses me? Yeah, I bet.* She shut down her email to focus on the manuscript. The last thing she needed was to lose her job due to Ryder's distractions.

The notification icon appeared on her screen. It beeped with each message she received. Every second that bloomin' thing beeped and it was driving her to distraction. She sighed. Who on God's green earth gave that man her email address? She'd kill him. Or her.

Ignoring that noise was dang near impossible. She searched her computer looking for a way to disable it. She was useless when it came to operating those crazy apps. If this noise continued, her co-workers were going to hit her over the head with a blunt object, pack her body in cement, and throw her in the ocean.

She searched everywhere for the disable button with no further luck. Then it dawned on her that she could mute her computer. She smiled at herself for being so clever. A push of a button and she no longer heard that annoying beep.

Ryder was officially being ignored. She mentally patted herself on the back. Now to get on the ball and finish the edits on this book. She opened the document, again, and set to work. She was never disappointed with this author. His work was always fresh and nearly polished to perfection upon arrival to her desk.

She was so engrossed in her work that she didn't hear her name being called. When a hand waved between her and her computer screen it took everything in her not to scream. Her hand flew to her chest, over her heart. Looking up into the eyes of the one that startled her she said, "Dang it Todd, you scared the snot out of me."

He shook his head at her wittiness. "Someone's here to see you."

"Oh. Would you tell them I'll be right there?"

"Sure." He walked away.

She made a few notes on her notepad, closed down the document, and made her way to the lobby. When she rounded the corner she stopped cold. He was standing at the window, his back to her, peering at the people walking along the sidewalk.

She didn't need to see his face to know who he was. His broad shoulders, dark messy hair, and that crazy black fingerless glove told her exactly who was waiting for her. "Go home, Ryder."

She turned to walk away but stopped at the sound of her name leaving his lips. "Cassie Sophia Strong. Sit and talk to me."

"I have work to do. You know, it's that thing that most of us have to do in order to pay our bills." She heard his footsteps, felt his presence when he stopped just a breath away from her back. "I have a deadline to meet," she said as a means of dismissal.

His hand rested on her shoulder. Her heart was torn. Should she continue on to her cubicle, leaving him behind, to avoid having her heart broken yet again? Or, she could stay and talk, risking the chance of her heart breaking once more.

He could see her conflicting emotions. She wanted to stay but she also wanted to go. It had taken him a great deal but he finally convinced his best friend, Jared, to spill the beans about Cassie's relationship status. To his surprise, she wasn't married nor was she dating. A big plus for him. "Don't you miss me at all?" he asked. His lips brushed her ear as he spoke.

"Whether or not I miss you isn't the issue." She stomped her foot as she finally turned to face him.

"Okay. What is the issue?" He searched her eyes.

Cassie had no idea how to handle this situation. Her heart, though it had mended to a certain degree, had not healed even a fraction. "I just can't."

She walked away before he could see the tears that formed and spilled over.

Chapter Five

The rest of the day proved to be unproductive. After Ryder's visit there was no way she could concentrate on her work. Her thoughts wouldn't leave him. She wanted nothing more than to give in to his demands, to spend time with him…to fall in love all over again.

On her way home from work, Cassie drove to the movie rental down the road from her house. After the day she had she needed a good romantic comedy to wind down. What she longed for was that day when she could take a vacation. But with bills to pay, that would have to wait.

Cassie was a regular there. She rented movies three to four times a week. The employee standing behind the counter waved at her as she walked in the store. She waved back and headed for the romantic comedy section. There were many to choose from but she always ended up with the same movie, Pretty Woman.

She laid the movie on the counter along with Twizzlers and a Coke. The employee scanned them and smiled. "You know, you've rented this movie so many times. Why don't you just buy a copy?"

Cassie laughed. With the money she spent renting this movie every week she could have already owned several copies. "That's okay, Sarah. If I bought every movie I loved then you wouldn't see me around much."

Sarah laughed. This was true. Cassie came in here nearly every day. Her presence alone brightened up the place. They had become friends because of Cassie's love for movies. "You're right."

Sarah didn't have to tell Cassie how much she owed, she knew it by heart. Cassie handed Sarah a five dollar bill and dropped the change into the donation box for the children's hospital. "So tell me about this book you're writing. Have you finished it yet?"

Sarah blushed, her cheeks a pretty shade of pink. "I'm close but I am so not ready to share it with anyone yet."

Cassie raised an eyebrow at her friend. "Come on now. You told me you were writing a book the last time I was in here. You can't just leave a girl hanging."

Two days ago when Cassie came in to rent a movie Sarah told her about the book she was writing. It was her first book and she was extremely nervous about it, afraid that no one would like it. She was afraid that it'd be an epic fail.

Sarah was a little worried about sharing her writing with Cassie. She knew that Cassie worked at a publishing company. "I have roughly twenty pages left. When it's done I will email it to you. I promise."

Cassie smiled. "Good. I'm glad to hear that."

The two chatted for a while longer. This was the reason she didn't buy her movies, she enjoyed coming in after a hard day's work and talking with the girls that ran the store. Cassie gathered her things, waved goodbye to Sarah, and left.

The sound of someone giggling drew her attention to the couple standing a few cars down from hers. She immediately regretted looking. The girl sat on the hood of a Mercedes SL running her fingers through the messy dark brown hair of none other than Ryder. Dang, there go her emotions running wild and free.

She couldn't help but watch their flirtation. It sickened her but she was unable to look away. She watched as he kissed the girl before helping her down off of his car. *Look away, look away, look away*, she shouted to herself mentally.

She finally did look away but not before he caught her staring. Great, now he would make a big deal out of her staring and find a way to use it against her. He said something to the pretty redhead he was with. She nodded her head like a crazed teenage fan. Then she kissed his cheek before entering the store, alone.

Ryder jogged toward her. "Cass, I need to talk to you."

Cassie fumbled with her keys, trying to open the car door and leave before he could say another word. She finally got it unlocked and rushed to get inside.

He caught hold of the door, preventing her from shutting it. She glared up at him. "Look, Ryder." She buckled her seatbelt. "I don't have time. Why don't you go back to your girlfriend and leave me alone. No more emails while I'm working either. Oh, and definitely no more stopping in at my place of employment."

Ryder crouched down so that they were eye level. "Fine, I won't email you while you're at work but I would like to talk to you. It's been a long time."

"Yes it has, but whose fault is that?" Cassie squeezed her hand into a tight fist causing her fingernails to bite into her flesh. The pain kept her from crying and making a total and complete fool of herself.

He sensed her agitation. "Can I stop by later?"

"I prefer you didn't." She put the keys in the ignition hoping he'd get the hint and walk away. "Anyway, wouldn't your girlfriend get mad at you for spending time alone with me?"

He rolled his eyes. "I'll be by in a couple of hours." He smiled at the angry puff of air she blew out, but she had said *I prefer you didn't* not *no*. He chucked her under the chin. "By the way, she's not my girlfriend. I don't have time for relationships. Big rock star, remember?" He stood, waved, and walked away.

Chapter Six

Jared managed to talk Cassie into coming to the house for a barbeque. It took a lot of persuasion to convince her to come. She was afraid of having to sit in the same room as Ryder. And the last thing that she wanted was to potentially see him with his date.

It wasn't until he promised that it would just be the three of them, no Ryder, that she finally caved in. He looked at his watch. She should have been here fifteen minutes ago.

"Quit fidgeting." Allie placed a kiss on Jared's cheek.

"She's late," he said looking at the time again.

"She'll be here." She made a point to wave her cell phone in front of him. "She texted me and said she was stopping at the store for dessert."

"I just want these two to sit down and talk." He put his arm around her waist, pulling her in for a deep tongue dancing kiss.

"As do I." She handed him the keys to their car. "You better head to the store if you plan on cooking a feast out back."

After a very long day at work and her run in with Ryder, Cassie decided to take Jared up on his offer and spend the evening with him and Allie. "We are not watching Pretty Woman," Allie demanded, hands on her hips. "You need to relax, have some fun." She sauntered across the room, turning on the stereo.

She rummaged through her collection of CDs until she found what she was looking for. It was very old school but definitely a goodie. She put the CD in the player. As soon as *Wannabe* poured out of the speakers Cassie laughed. She hadn't heard that song in a very long time.

Allie made a come here motion with her index finger. Cassie shook her head but then tossed the movie onto the coffee table and joined her friend. The two of them danced around the living room singing. It felt great. Cassie could feel the pent up stress melting away. When the song ended Cassie hit the replay button.

They were having so much fun, neither one of them heard the front door open. Jared stood in the doorway, grocery bag in hand. Those two looked so beautiful, goofy but beautiful. He silently watched, not wanting to ruin their moment of happiness.

The song ended and Allie spun Cassie around. Her eyes landed on Jared. A deep blush colored her cheeks. "Oh-Mylanta, next time warn a girl." She spun on her heel and turned off the stereo.

Allie rushed to her boyfriend, giving him a wet kiss. He embraced her for a moment. "I bought some steaks for the grill."

"Nice." Allie peeked into the bag. "Yum, you bought baked beans, potato salad, and coleslaw."

"Sure did." He looked at Cassie. "I bought plenty of potato salad just for you."

Cassie smiled. "Hey you don't have to ask me twice. Steak sounds great and I love you for the potato salad."

"Good. Then I'll go get the grill started." He headed towards the back door.

The girls gathered plates, cups, and a pitcher of iced tea. They carried them outside to the large picnic table. Allie turned on the pool lights so they could enjoy the pool while Jared grilled their meat.

Cassie didn't have to worry about a bathing suit. Allie kept plenty in the pool house in case they had a visitor that needed one. That visitor was usually Cassie. "You should wear this one." Allie held up a bright orange bikini.

"No way." Cassie could not force herself to wear a bikini. She had too many blemishes she'd rather no one else see.

"Come on, it's just us." Allie held the little pieces of fabric out to her.

Cassie stood firm. She shook her head and grabbed a full piece bathing suit. She ignored Allie's insistence on the two piece and her friend's claim that she was not as flawed as she thought she was. When she had changed, she walked around a pouting Allie. "I'll wait for you in the pool."

"You're no fun," Allie called out as Cassie shut the door behind her.

The moment Cassie stepped foot out of the pool house, the smells from the grill hit her nose. Her mouth watered, anticipating what was to come. She passed Jared and the mouth watering grill. Climbing up onto the diving board, she dove into the cool waters below.

Allie exited the pool house minutes after Cassie. She was about to join her friend in the pool when the back door swung open.

Cassie was in the far corner of the pool, her arms stretched out on the edges. She relaxed against the side of the pool, letting her body float freely. When Ryder strode out of the back door her heart skipped a beat. Some part of her was happy to see him. Though she tried to stop it, a small smile tugged at the corner of her lips.

Her emotions were a roller coaster of a ride. She couldn't fathom why she'd be happy to see his face. She had harbored resentment for all these years and at the sight of him, her heart was willing to push those feelings aside.

Even after all that time apart he still had some kind of hold on her. Something that made her heart beat to a crazy rhythm.

Sadly, her moment of excitement didn't last long. The moment that bubbly redhead stepped outside and snuggled into Ryder's side, her smile died.

This was why she tried so hard to stay away from him. Because regardless of how much her heart longed for him, he couldn't commit. So being angry was easier, it protected her heart from acting on impulse with him which would lead to her destruction.

Ryder snaked his arm around her shoulders. At his touch the girl laughed. Not a giggle like most girls. No, this was a freak show of a laugh. Ms. Bubbly redhead sounded more like a hyena than a woman.

Allie and Jared share a horrified look. They had planned on getting Ryder and Cassie under the same roof, but they didn't predict that he'd bring a date. The boy had only been in town a couple of days, one would think that was too soon to be out prowling for chicks.

Cassie saw the exchange between Jared and Allie and wondered if that look was because of her or because of hyena girl. Ryder leaned close to her, saying something in her ear, and she laughed again. This time it sounded more of a mixture of a hyena and a witch. What did he see in her?

Cassie watched as Ryder swatted her on the backside. She was not going to sit here all night and watch his endless flirting with this girl. Her heart had already been chewed up, spit out, and thrown in a grinder. It had taken her years to put the pieces back together.

Jared cleared his throat, loudly. When Ryder failed to pay attention Jared spoke. "Have you no manners, man?"

"What?" Ryder stopped his groping long enough to look at his friend. Jared nodded in Cassie's direction. Ryder followed his friend's gaze and froze. His eyes grew as large as saucers. "Oh."

"Yeah." Jared shook his head at his friend's stupidity.

Cassie climbed out of the pool. She'd forgotten to bring a towel with her. With water dripping from her hair and rolling down her skin, she walked right past Ryder and hyena girl.

She heard him calling her name but chose to ignore him. Protecting herself was top priority.

She entered the pool house. Forget dinner, she'd get take out and go home. She hung the bathing suit up on a hook to drip dry. Smoothing her blouse and skirt out, she opened the door. "I better go. I have a ton of work to do before tomorrow."

Allie's face fell, her shoulders slumped. "At least stay and eat."

"Maybe next time." She avoided Ryder's stare as she headed towards the house. She heard his footsteps but continued on her way hoping he'd just give up. No such luck.

He reached out for her arm, halting her before she could reach the handle to the back door. "Cass…" For once he was at a loss for words.

"Hey." She didn't turn to look at him. "I have a lot of work waiting for me. I need to go. It was nice seeing you though."

"Can I stop by later?"

Cassie turned on her heel. She looked over his shoulder at hyena girl who was calling out his name, or rather, screeching out his name. Ryder, unfazed by her shrill voice, pleaded with his eyes. "Get back to your date. I really need to leave."

He glanced over his shoulder then turned his attention back to her. "Give me an hour to get her back home and I'll drop by. I really would like to catch up. I've missed you."

"Yeah, I can tell." She jerked her arm free and continued into the house. Her keys were lying on top of the movie she'd brought over. Hyena girl yelled louder, earning her repulsive glares from both Jared and Allie.

Ryder fell in step right behind her, his date just background noise in his ears. If he'd known that Cassie would be here he'd have never brought that girl with him. Heck, if he'd known that she was so annoying he would have never accepted a date from her. He couldn't stand the way she laughed or her high-pitched yelling.

To be perfectly honest, Cassie was the one he wanted to spend his free time with. Let's face it, you don't love someone the way he loved her back in high school and not carry a torch for that person. Their lives may have moved in different directions but he still very much loved her.

Retrieving her movie and keys, she waltzed out of the house. He stood in the doorway. "I'll be there in an hour, two max." She pretended not to hear him.   She drove away without a backwards glance.

Chapter Seven

"How the heck was I to know that the idiot would bring a flipping date?" Jared asked.

He and Allie had planned this barbeque while plotting ways to get Ryder and Cassie together. Those two had some issues that needed to be worked out. What they didn't expect was for Ryder to bring a girl to the festivities.

"There you are. I was wondering where everyone ran off to." Ryder's date came waltzing into the kitchen looking around, presumably for her man.

Both Jared and Allie rolled their eyes. Neither one of them could stand her screeching racket she called a voice.

Ryder strolled into the kitchen after watching Cassie drive away. The moment he came into view his date ran to his side. "There you are, love. I've been looking everywhere for you. Come on," she tugged on his arm, "let's go for a dip in the pool."

He gently removed his arm from her grip.

The girl was persistent. She reached for his hand, tugging him towards the back door. "Come on."

He pulled away again. "Change of plans, babe." Looking at Jared he asked, "Can I get her number from you?"

Jared sent a text to Ryder with Cassie's home phone and cell phone numbers.

Ryder glanced at his phone. "Thanks, man." Placing his hand on the small of her back, Ryder ushered his date out of the house. He'd drop her off and then head over to Cassie's. Hopefully this visit would go better than the last one.

If Cassie allowed herself to spend any kind of time with Ryder then she'd end up falling madly in love with him all over again and that frightened her. It frightened her because there was no way that she could sit back and be second place to his groupies. And if he did manage to commit to her while he was in town, it wouldn't last. Eventually, his manager would call with the next tour schedule and he'd leave.

She contemplated turning off every light in the house in hopes that he'd think she wasn't home.

Her car was hidden in the garage, it could work. *Knock, knock.* She silently cursed. That's what happens when you try to weigh out your options at the last minute, you run out of time.

She peeked out of the peephole. He wore a black shirt and his ripped faded blue jeans. She also noticed that he was not wearing his ridiculous glove. That was a surprise.

She held her breath and didn't move a muscle. If she was quiet then he might just go away. *Knock, knock.* This time his knock was a little louder.

He looked at the peephole. It appeared that he looked right at her. "I know you're in there." She still refused to make a sound or open the door. His stare became intense, like he could actually see her from that side of the peephole.

Taking a deep breath, she stepped back and opened the door. "Sorry, I was busy."

Ryder walked past her. "Sure you were." He wandered around her living room, looking at her photos. There was one that caught his eye right away, a young boy with Cassie and her brother Nathan. Another photo stuck out, it was a picture of him on stage at his first concert. He was shocked that she'd even have that one.

Cassie cleared her throat. "You came over to talk not to inspect my house."

"Right." He sat on the sofa. "So how have you been?"

Cassie stared at him opened mouth. When he said he wanted to talk to her she figured he'd say something to the extent of *I'm here to retrieve all my CD's and whatever else I left with you.* She did not expect him to come waltzing in making small talk.

"Okay." He leaned forward, resting his arms on his knees. "What's your problem? I thought that you would be excited to see me. You've been nothing but rude."

"My problem?" She sat down in a chair across the room from him. "Why did you come back, Ryder?"

He stared at her, lost for words. Really, what had crawled up her butt anyway? She was so rude. He did a quick shake of his head to clear his thoughts before answering her question. "My tour is over and I thought I could use a break. I haven't had a vacation since, well, ever."

"Yeah, me neither," she cut him off. Why did this have to be so hard? Her heart hurt so badly just being in the same room with him because even through the heartache, her heart belonged to him. She fought the tears that threatened to reveal themselves. "Why are you here?" She pointed to a spot on the living room floor as to emphasize where here was.

He looked down at the spot she pointed to then back at her, confused. "I came to see you. I thought that you might actually be happy to see me." His hazel eyes bore into hers. "What is wrong with you?"

"You left me," she shouted. She hadn't meant to say it. It made her sound so childish and she hated herself for it. He looked at her, taken aback by her outburst. She stood. "We had just graduated high school. We were planning on getting an apartment together and starting the new chapter of our lives."

"Yes we did but our plans changed. You always knew that it was a possibility," he shot back.

She shook with rage, her cheeks heating with boiling anger. Did he not understand a flipping thing? She had loved him, would have traveled to the ends of the earth just to be with him.

Tears formed in her eyes and she fought hard to keep them at bay.

When she managed to swallow the lump in her throat, she continued. "When you came to see me that night you said that you had just signed a contract with a record label and were leaving the next day." She turned away from him. "You just packed up and left town."

"Dang woman, you're still upset over that?" He stood, crossed the room to her. "I had a once in a lifetime opportunity. I couldn't pass that up." He turned her to face him. "You knew that was my dream when we got together." After all, it wasn't like they were married with a family at the time he received the offer to tour the world.

Unable to stop herself, she blinked and the tears fell from her eyes. "Yes, I did." She wiped her eyes with the collar of her shirt. "I guess I had just hoped that I would be a part of that dream."

She walked around him. If she didn't find a tissue soon her nose would start dripping.

He couldn't believe his ears. At the time that he made his decision to leave, she was also pursuing a dream of her own. "If I remember correctly, you were planning to pursue the publishing industry."

The publishing field had been a dream of hers since she could remember. When they graduated high school she'd already had her classes scheduled for the fall. He was right. She was also pursuing her own dreams at the time.

It had taken a lot of work to land a job at Bradshaw Publishing. She started out answering phones and running errands. After a few months of running errands Mr. Bradshaw called her into his office.

One of his editors had just quit and he was in search of a replacement. He was reluctant but decided to give her a small article to edit. When she turned it in, he was impressed by her skills and gave her the position on a trial bases.

She started to walk away but Ryder took hold of her hand, tugging her body close to his. He ran his fingers through her silky blonde hair. "Man, I've missed this." Leaning forward, he pressed his lips to hers.

Cassie was stunned by his actions. She tried to fight it but her heart out won her mind. After eight years of absence, he still made her heart beat wildly. She found herself kissing him back, wrapping her arms around his neck. The moment was beautiful, until his cell phone rang.

He pulled away, leaving her cold from the loss of his touch. He fished in his pocket for the phone. He didn't even read the name on the Caller ID, he just hit answer. "Hello?" He listened to the caller for a minute. "I can't talk right now."

Cassie looked at him, the man she had loved since her freshman year of high school. No amount of time had changed that. She knew that she needed to tell him now while she had the chance, he deserved to know.

Ryder moved to the kitchen for some privacy. When he was out of sight she touched her kiss swollen lips with her fingertips. Her heart beat furiously with these raw emotions, until she heard his next words. "Listen Baby, I don't have time to talk right now. I have this thing in the morning and I need to go."

Baby? Oh, well that was just great. Then again, she shouldn't have been too surprised. Earlier she saw him with that redhead making out in the middle of the movie rental parking lot. The same girl he took to Jared's house, parading around like his little trophy. So he *was* the typical rock star.

This would be the death of her if she didn't nip this fling, this one night stand or whatever she was to him, in the bud.

Cassie glared at him when he entered the living room. "Who was that?" She did her best not to sound like a jealous girlfriend. After all they weren't a couple and hadn't been for a very long time. Gawd, she needed a vacation.

"Oh, it was just a member of the other band I was touring with." He reached out to touch her face but she backed away. "Cass, what's up?" He looked confused by her reaction.

Lies. He was willing to tell her a lie about his call? "I think you should go." She pointed to the front door. "Don't come back Ryder, please," she whispered. Her heart couldn't go through these yo-yo emotions any more. If he didn't want to be with her, and only her, then he needed to stay away for good.

Ryder stared at her, stunned. One minute everything was great and the next minute she was as cold as ice. What the heck. Her bipolar attitude was starting to give him whiplash.

He opened his mouth to speak but snapped it shut instead. He couldn't handle this kind of craziness. Without saying bye he walked out the door, slamming it shut behind him.

Chapter Eight

Ryder slammed the door to his Mercedes. What in the world had just happened back there? Cassie kissed him, just like old times, but then she went all psycho and ordered him out. He stomped across the yard and up the porch steps.

The front door opened before he could reach out for the knob. Jared greeted him with an ice cold beer. "Here man, looks like you could use this."

"Thanks." He sat on the top step, popped the top and took a long drink. "I know you were waiting for me. How'd you know I needed it?"

Jared stepped outside, sitting on the porch with Ryder. "Allie. Cassie called her when you left her place."

"What the heck is that girl's problem? One minute she's kissing me." Jared raised a brow at this bit of information. Allie hadn't mentioned that to him earlier. "Then the next minute she's ordering me to leave and never come back." Ryder tipped the bottle, draining the beer.

Jared sighed. "Look, a lot has changed since you left." He sipped on his beer before continuing. "You need to be patient with her. Life hasn't been easy for that girl."

"Oh and it's been so easy for me," he huffed. "Sleeping while on tour is dang near impossible. Between practice and concerts I barely have enough time to eat." He couldn't believe his own ears. That statement sounded very much like a pout, even to him.

"I'm sure there were plenty of women to help relieve some of your stress," Jared teased.

"Well, yeah, there were women." Ryder smiled. Jared hit the nail on the head. There had definitely been plenty of women to keep him company. Here recently there was a female guitarist in the band that he had just finished touring with.

Jared drained his beer. "Don't string Cassie along. She deserves better than that, a player is definitely not what she needs. Her life has changed dramatically since you left, she needs stability." Jared stood up, said good night, and went in the house.

Ryder didn't know what to think. Cassie seemed to be doing well. She had a great job in a publishing company just like she always wanted. Besides, what was wrong with reliving some of their past romance?

She didn't have a ring on that finger of hers or any children for that matter. The way he saw it, they were both consenting adults. If she wanted to get a little freaky with him, what business was that of anyone else?

He sat his empty bottle down. Coming home was the right move. Not only was he able to visit his friends, he was discovering something else. Cassie was still the number one girl in his life. The one that played his heartstrings to perfection.

Chapter Nine

After Ryder's visit, Cassie had a restless night's sleep. Her dreams were a mixture of nightmares and what-might-have-been.

What might have been if Ryder had chosen her over music? The two of them might be living in a nice home with children running around. Most importantly, his arms would be around her every night.

Then the nightmare would kick in. They were no longer happy, their relationship only lasting for a couple of years because he grew to resent her for staying. He ended up hating her for choosing her instead of his dream.

What might have been if she would have given up everything to follow him on tour? It would have been rough and very tiring but she would still have his arms around her every night.

Then like clockwork the nightmare reared its ugly head, right when she felt safe in his arms. This time her dream Ryder didn't pack up and leave, he just brought his groupies back to the tour bus not bothering to hide them from her. Her dream Ryder would smirk at her as she watched, horrified, while he made out with random fans.

The next morning Cassie woke with the biggest headache. The lack of rest made her grumpy and unpleasant to be around. Work was slow going which only irked her nerves more.

Finally the clock struck twelve and she packed up her things to meet Allie for lunch.

The two of them met at the café across the street from Bradshaw Publishing. "Jeez Cassie," Allie said as she sat down in the booth. "You look like you've been hit by a truck."

Cassie removed her massaging hands from her temples and popped more Ibuprofen. "Oh thanks." She sipped her coffee. Today was proving to be a very long day and only promised to get worse. "I didn't sleep well last night. I really wish he would have stayed gone. It definitely would be easier if he had."

"Have you even attempted to have that conversation with him?" The waitress came over to their table. Allie ordered an iced tea and asked for a few more minutes to look over the menu.

"I have but the last thing I want or need is to drag up all of those old feelings." Cassie thought back to the night before when Ryder had kissed her. The chemistry was still there. Her feelings for him were still very much there.

"I understand where you're coming from I really do, but you need to sit down and talk to him." Allie tapped her manicured nails on the tabletop. "What you're doing isn't fair. Set things straight or this will all come back to bite you in the butt."

"And tell him what? He's going to leave just as soon as his manager calls with the next big tour anyway." The waitress came back and Allie ordered a Grilled Chicken Caesar salad. Cassie, on the other hand, needed more than a salad to get her through the day. She ordered a bacon cheese burger with extra fries.

"Okay, I get it. I do, but he deserves the truth." Allie's phone buzzed with a text. With a goofy smile like that, it could only be one person.

Jared. "Jared is having a party this weekend. Please come."

Cassie shook her head. Being at a party with Ryder just wasn't what she needed. The waitress brought their food to the table and topped off Cassie's coffee.

"Come on. You can't avoid him forever." Allie took a bite of her salad, dabbing the dressing off of her lower lip.

"Is he bringing another girl? I will think about it as long as he is dateless. I don't think I could handle watching him grope some hot chick in front of me." Cassie knew she sounded like a high school girl but she couldn't help it. Ryder was the first and only love of her life. Whether he knew it or not, he still held her heart in the palm of his hands. There had never been anyone else for her.

"Goodie. Be there Friday at seven, we'll make sure Ryder doesn't bring anyone else."

The two finished their lunch, chatting about television shows and books. Neither one of them knew it but sitting outside, in a vehicle parked on the curb, someone was watching them. Cassie was being observed, and not for the first time.

Chapter Ten

Ryder nearly choked on his Coke. "What do you mean I can't bring any girls to the party? I dang sure ain't bringing a dude." He shuddered at the image now clogging his brain.

Allie smiled sickeningly sweet, so much so that Ryder wanted to wipe it off of her face. "I invited Cassie and I do not want you throwing some chick in her face." She turned and left the room.

Ryder watched Allie leave. He looked at Jared who just shrugged his shoulders. "Hey, I'm not gonna argue with that." He too left the room.

Ryder moved to stand in front of the window unit. The cold air blowing on his back felt wonderful in this blistering hot house. He'd have to go out and buy his friend a central unit. These little window coolers did zero to cool down the house.

How they lived here was beyond him. To him it made absolutely no sense to live in a house that had a large pool and a pool house but no central air inside the main house. Why have the luxury items outside if you didn't have them inside?

If he'd known how ridiculously hot it would be in this house he would have never asked to stay here while he was in town. He brought his ice cold Coke can to his forehead. The coolness helped lower his temperature, just a smidge.

He sat on the arm of the sofa, the cool air blowing in his face, reflecting on tonight's discussion. First of all, he wasn't sure how he felt about being bossed around like a child. He was a grown man and those two had no right to treat him this way, they were all the same age for crying out loud. That behavior would wear on his nerves quick.

He made a mental note to talk to them later about all of that. Right now he had more exciting things to think about. His friends were having a party Friday night. He'd get to see a few people he hadn't seen since high school.

The one thing that brought a wicked smile to his face was Cassie. She was going to be here Friday evening. He couldn't wait.

He thought about Allie's demand. No problem. If Cassie was going to be here then he didn't want any other girl to keep him company anyway. In fact, since he'd been back, Cassie was the only girl entertaining his thoughts.

Sure he was still attracted to pretty women but the more he saw Cassie, the more he thought of her, and the more he found his interest in those other women diminishing. He didn't want a random woman in his arms. He wanted Cassie.

She was his drug of choice. He'd do whatever he had to do just to get her back in his arms again. Her eyes alone beckoned him like a siren song. Having a relationship would prove to be difficult with his profession but if she was willing, they could enjoy one another while he was here in town.

Chapter Eleven

Friday night rolled around and Cassie was more nervous than ever, which was ridiculous considering she was a grown woman. She shouldn't be nervous about going to a party that Ryder would be at. She checked herself over in the mirror one more time before heading out the door.

She contemplated turning around several times before reaching Jared and Allie's home. She pulled into the driveway. There were a couple of people there already, the music was loud enough for a party but not too noisy to bother the neighbors.

She drummed her fingertips on the steering wheel. If she left now she could rent a movie, pop some popcorn, and curl up on the sofa. A tap on her window startled her out of her thoughts.

Ryder waved and pointed to the lock. Instead of unlocking her door she rolled down the window. The hot summer air hit her in the face causing her to take in a quick breath. The terrible thing about living in Texas during the summer was the evening temperatures were just as hot and muggy as the daytime temperatures, there was no respite.

"What do you want, Ryder?" She wasn't in the mood for his charms.

"I just thought I'd escort you inside." Once again he pointed to the lock. "But you will have to unlock the car door first."

If she put the car in reverse she might even have a chance to run over his foot on her way out.

Her foot hovered over the brake, her hand on the shift handle. She needed to get away, to protect her heart. Light flooded the yard as Allie opened the front door.

One look at her friend and Cassie knew she couldn't leave. Her friend waved frantically, she was excited to have her here. "Fine." She rolled up the window and unlocked the car door.

Ryder opened her door and held out his hand. Ignoring his outstretched hand, she stepped out of the car. He shut the door and she locked it. "I'm glad you came. I'd like to talk to you some more."

"Not interested." She picked up speed. She embraced Allie in a hug and informed her that she would have to leave early. Allie knew that Cassie used her editing deadlines as a way to avoid spending too much time in the same house as Ryder.

Allie hoped that the two of them would just sit down and talk. Neither of them may know it but they were meant to be, their names were written in the stars. She knew this back when they were in high school, which was why she pushed them together way back then.

They were created to complete the other. Some people called it soul mates. Whatever the case, those two were destined for one another. If they needed a little help along the way then she'd be more than happy to push them in the right direction. Again.

"Ryder, why don't you get Cassie some punch?" Allie shooed him away with a wave of her hand.

Cassie leaned her head on her friend's shoulder. "I'm not sure this is a good idea. You know what I went through the first time."

"Yes, I remember. This time though, you're both older. Things will be okay. You'll see." Allie ushered her in the house and shut the door behind them.

Other than Jared and Allie there were two other couples there. The DJ switched tracks and played *Come Over*, her favorite country song.

Allie grabbed her by the hand, dragging her to the center of the room. "Dance with me."

Ryder came back into the room in time to see Cassie and Allie singing and swaying to the music. That was the sexiest thing he had ever seen. He didn't like country music but he could grow to love this song, especially when Cassie was singing along to it.

He leaned against the wall, watching. The lyrics were great and spoke just how he felt. He wondered if Cassie would warm his bed again. He still loved her but his life didn't allow room for a real relationship.

The song ended and he approached her with a cup in hand. "I didn't know you could sing so well."

"I can't." She sipped the punch. Good, no alcohol. "Thanks," she said raising her cup. "This is good."

"You bet." A slow song came on and he asked, "May I?"

Cassie knew that accepting a dance with him was dangerous. She shook her head. "I don't think that's a good idea."

"Why?" he asked, reaching out to caress her arm. "Aren't we both adults?"

"We are." His touch caused goose bumps to break out on her arms. She couldn't fathom how she could be so torn where he was concerned. But as much as she wanted to save herself, he was slowly chipping away at that stone wall she had around her heart.

Unable to stop herself she nodded. His hands firmly gripped her waist, gently pulling her flush up against him. Her arms wrapped around his shoulders, her cup dangling from her fingertips.

His breath against her neck sent shivers down her spine. She closed her eyes, letting the music lead her. Soon they moved in synch with one another, their bodies swaying to the music. That one moment was all it took for the world around them to get lost, for time to stop.

Everything and everyone around them could no longer be seen or heard. Here in this moment it was just the two of them and the music. The music was the hypnotic thread that held them in their own little universe.

She was so lost in her dance with Ryder that she never noticed when Allie gently pried the cup from her hand. She could no longer fight this attraction. Being here like this felt so right. This moment with Ryder and these butterflies fluttering in her stomach, it reminded her of a time when she was truly happy.

Ryder leaned his head forward, touching his forehead to hers. Every alarm in her head rang loudly, warning her that the wall around her heart was on the verge of crumbling to the ground.

His hazel eyes penetrated hers. All the love she harbored for him resurfaced, overriding the alarm bells that rang in the forefront of her mind. He was the only guy for her. Maybe giving him a chance wouldn't be such a bad thing.

The music changed. He grinned at her when *I'll Make Love To You* played over the speakers. It was a song that he used to play for her, especially when they were about to make love. They continued to sway to the music even as he backed them out of the room and down the hallway.

His hands caressed her lower back, then her arms until they made their way to her face. With a hand on either side of her face he leaned forward, tenderly pressing his lips to hers. His soft smooth lips were heaven, lighting her insides on fire.

She melted into his kiss. Yes, she had most definitely missed this. He guided her into his bedroom, kicking the door closed behind him. The moonlight shone through the window providing enough light to see. He toed off his shoes, lifted her off her feet, and carried her to the bed.

He unfastened the button of her jean shorts followed by the zipper. Sliding his hand along the flat of her stomach he lightly caressed her navel. He loved the way she shivered and broke out in goose bumps at his touch.

He stopped when he felt the change in her skin. He glanced down but didn't notice anything. The moonlight wasn't bright enough to see the imperfection that he assumed was a tiny scar on her abdomen. The instant he ran his finger along the scar she bolted up off the bed, fastening her shorts. "I need to leave. We'll talk later. I promise."

He sat up, stunned. What the heck just happened? Surely she wasn't embarrassed over a silly little scar. He wouldn't look at her differently just because she had an imperfection right below her navel.

Chapter Twelve

"You're going to have to tell him sooner or later." Allie added more lotion to her legs before reclining on her beach towel. They were a long way from the beach but the local pool was just as good as the beach when it came to sun tanning.

"I know." Cassie rolled onto her back. "I'm just scared."

"Well, honey, you need to let go of that fear." She gave Cassie a sideways glance. "He's bound to find out and the last thing you want is for him to find out from someone else."

Cassie thought about that for a minute. Allie was right. He would find out soon and it should come from her. She just couldn't get over the fear of him hating her, and she knew that he would when he learned the truth.

"I know that. I just don't want him to hate me." She blew hair out of her face.

"I doubt very much that he'd hate you. He might be ticked off at you but that would eventually blow over."

"I promise to tell him soon. I just need to build up the courage." Cassie adjusted her sunglasses. "On a happy note, he called me last night and we had a nice long chat."

"Yeah, I know. My walls are thin, remember?" Allie giggled. "It reminded me of high school all over again listening to you guys talk on the phone until all hours of the night."

"It was nice. I apologized for taking off like a bat out of hell. Poor guy had no clue what he'd done. I had to reassure him that he didn't do anything wrong, I just wasn't ready to move forward so quickly."

"Good. I'm glad that the two of you are finally talking."

Her cell phone rang. Cassie picked up the device. It was an out of state number. "Hello?"

"Hey Cass." That deep throaty voice brought a smile to her face.

"Ryder?"

"Yeah, where are you on this beautiful Saturday afternoon?" In the background a keyboard and bass could be heard. "Forgive the noise I'm walking out of the studio."

Her smile faded. If he was in the studio already then he must be preparing his next album and that would mean his time here was limited. "I'm at the pool on Hunter's Parkway."

"It will take me at least thirty-five minutes to get there." A car door shut. "Will you still be there?"

"Yeah, we plan on going for swim after our tan anyway." She put her pointer finger to her lips when Allie gave her a very confused look.

"Great. I'll see you soon."

Cassie's grin lit up her face. "See you soon." She ended the call and laid the cell phone next to her on the towel.

Allie sat straight up. "We plan on going for a swim after we tan? Have you lost your mind? I thought we were going to catch a movie afterwards?" The three questions came out in one breath and Cassie wondered how she said so many words without gasping for air.

She shrugged her shoulders. "It was Ryder. What can I say?"

"Oh, well in that case," Allie said, "maybe I should call Jared to come pick me up. He can take me to the movies while you play catch up with the boy toy." She had been hoping and praying for these two to realize they belonged together, for eight long years she hoped and prayed.

Cassie raised one eyebrow. She wouldn't mind some alone time with Ryder. After last night he was the only thing occupying her mind. Secretly she hoped that he would remember just how much they loved each other before he left Texas to tour the world.

If he remembered the love they shared then maybe he'd decide to stay. Committing to her wouldn't mean the end of his career. They would simply have to learn how to work around his music.

The alarm on her phone went off, signaling that it was time to turn over. She rolled over onto her stomach. She couldn't wait until her time was up. She wanted to have a nice summer tan but this heat was taking her breath away.

"I'm glad you finally quit avoiding him." Allie rolled over. "Now you two can kiss and make up. Maybe you'll even get married in the very near future."

"Whoa." Cassie shifted so she could see her friend. "Nobody is talking about marriage. We just started talking after these last several years of absence. Besides, he was just leaving the studio when he called." She bit the inside of her cheek to keep her emotions in check. "You know what that means."

Allie's face fell, just for a brief moment. "Hey, that's who he is. The two of you can work around something as simple as music."

"I hope so." That had been her dream since she started dating Ryder back in high school. Back then he played in a garage band with a couple of friends. Later that garage band played in late night cafés and anywhere else teenage boys could get in to play.

She used to dream of the day she became the wife of a rock star. Only she pictured him playing locally. What a silly dream that was. None of it went as she had dreamed it would.

A shadow fell over her. She opened her eyes. A pair of black combat style chained boots stood just inches from her face. She looked up and saw Ryder, his hands behind his back. "That was fast, I just got off the phone with you a few minutes ago."

His expression was one of amusement. "It's been longer than that."

She turned her head to the side. Allie could confirm that it hadn't been more than five minutes. Except Allie wasn't there, her towel and cell phone were missing too. Cassie picked up her phone. Thirty minutes had passed since she'd turned on her stomach, thirty-five since she'd talked to Ryder.

She buried her face in her towel. She must have fallen asleep. "I didn't snore did I?" She was too afraid to look up.

"Oh yeah, it was like a freight train. You had these poor kids screaming for help because they thought you were some kind of monster that was going to eat them all." He laughed so hard his belly shook.

Cassie picked up her bottle of sun tan lotion and threw it at his chest. "Ha ha, you're so funny." She stood, wrapping the towel around her. "Let me change and we can leave if you want." It was then that she noticed his hands had not moved from behind his back. "What're you hiding?"

"Nothing. Go get dressed." He moved with every step she took to prevent her from seeing anything. She wanted to look so bad. He could see the desire on her face, not knowing was killing her. Patience was never her strong suit.

"Come on, you're hiding something. Let me see it." She tried to dash to the side, hoping she could get a glimpse before he moved it out of her sight again. No such luck.

"If you don't hurry up and change, I'm going to give this to someone else." He knew that would get her moving. It did too. She rushed out of the pool area like a speeding bullet.

She nearly tripped over her own two feet on her way to the changing room. It was a sight to see, and he loved every minute of it.

She was gone and back in record time. What'd she do, twitch her nose to magically dress herself? Bouncing like a giddy school girl, she pointed to his hidden hands. "So, what are you hiding?"

He brought one hand forward. A small stuffed bear sat in his palm. She was reminded of their first date. He had showed up on her parent's doorstep holding a small stuffed bear, a box of chocolates, and a single white rose.

Picking up the bear, she clutched it to her chest. "I love it. Thank you."

He brought his other hand forward. A bouquet of white roses greeted her. "I almost bought a box of chocolates but I figured they'd melt along the way."

Bringing the roses up to her nose, she inhaled. "They're beautiful. Thank you for these."

She linked her arm through his and followed him to the parking lot. Today was going to be a great day.

Chapter Thirteen

Ryder carried the two large bags of Chinese food from the Mercedes to Cassie's kitchen table. His cell phone vibrated in his jeans pocket. A quick peek at the Caller ID and he rolled his eyes. *Not now*, he thought.

Cheryl, the keyboard player for the band he toured with, was calling. Why couldn't this girl get a clue? He had no interest in her, none whatsoever. Sure they hooked up, quite a bit actually, while they were on the road but she knew that he wasn't committing to a relationship. She was just a friend with benefits type of girl to him. He was sure to make that perfectly clear their first night together.

He ended the call, not bothering to answer it. She had called every day, several times a day in fact, to tell him how much she missed him. This was getting way out of hand. Looking at his cell phone a thought occurred to him. He could always change his cell number. It's not like she knew where he lived or anything.

Cassie collected two plates from the cabinet. While she loaded them down with food his cell phone vibrated again. "I need to answer this call, do you mind?"

"No." She pointed down the hall. "First door on the left."

"I won't be long." He winked at her then smiled when a beautiful color of red crept along her neck and cheeks. She bowed her head, allowing her hair to hide the blush. Ryder admired her for just a minute before leaving the room. Gawd, she was beautiful.

His phone quit vibrating signaling that the call went to voicemail. Two seconds later it started up again. He shut the bedroom door and answered the phone. "What do you want, Cheryl?"

"Don't be rude to me, Ryder. I'm calling to tell you how much I miss you." Her sultry voice irked on his nerves like nails on a chalkboard.

"I don't have time for this. What do you want?" He ran his fingers along Cassie's dresser. It was the same dresser that they had planned on buying for their new apartment all those years ago. He was pleased to see that she had gone ahead with the purchase.

"Come on, Ryder," she cooed. "Baby, I'm lonely."

"Look, Cheryl, you need to quit calling me Baby." He sighed and took a deep breath. "Just quit calling me, period. We are not in a relationship, never have been." He cut her off when she started to protest. "Forget my number and leave me alone."

"What about our last night on tour? You told me that you were so glad that we were on tour together. You told me I was beautiful." The girl was near hysterics now.

Ryder thought back, trying to remember exactly what was said that night. He was pretty sure he didn't lead her on in any way. "I *was* glad that we toured together, we had a great time. And you are beautiful. But Cheryl, we were never dating. We both had needs that needed to be met and that's all that was, nothing more."

"Ryder, don't leave me," she wailed. "Please. I love you." She sobbed so heavily he could hardly understand her.

"I'm sorry," he paused, "but I don't love you." He felt bad for telling her this over the phone. These kinds of things should be done in person but she was in California and he was in Texas. "You're beautiful and bound to find another guy in no time."

"I don't want another guy, I want you." She blew her nose, not daintily like most women did. No, this was a loud horn blowing type of blow.

"I'm sorry." He didn't say another word, just ended the call and shut off his phone. What was he going to do with that girl? She was beginning to weird him out.

He joined Cassie at the table. She had given him most of the egg rolls. A huge grin appeared on his face. She remembered how much he loved those things. "Everything okay?" she asked.

"Yes, everything's just fine." He tossed his cell phone on the table and dug in. It had been so long since he'd had any decent Chinese food. His mouth watered the instant the egg roll touched his tongue. The delightful flavors brought a moan out of him. He leaned back in the chair to savor the bite.

"You're such a dork." She picked up a noodle from her plate and threw it at him. The look of shock on his face as the noodle landed across his nose made her laugh.

"Oh, how very ladylike," he teased. He took another bite of his egg roll, making sure to be a little more dramatic this time. Once he was done making a total fool of himself, he continued, "You're lucky that I'm starving and these are delicious, otherwise you'd be wearing some Kung Pao chicken in your hair."

She giggled. It was beginning to feel like old times. The only problem was; would she be strong enough to watch him go when his manager said it was time to pack up and move on? Probably not but she would worry about that day when it arrived. Right now she was going to enjoy every minute she had with him.

After dinner Ryder followed Cassie out to the patio. Even though it was dark out, the heat and humidity were still high. Not a very comfortable atmosphere to be sitting in but one that he would endure to be near her.

"Here." She handed him a glass of iced tea.

He sipped his tea as he watched her dust off two patio chairs. When she was done he sat down on a chair and pulled the other chair right up next to his. They gazed at the stars until their glasses were empty.

"Ryder?" Cassie leaned forward, glancing sideways at him. "Do you have your guitar with you?"

He nodded. He carried his baby with him everywhere he went. "It's in the trunk."

She ran her finger along the top of her glass. "Would you play for me?"

He smiled. It had been a long time since he'd played the guitar for her. "You bet." He set his glass down on the table and left to retrieve his guitar.

When he returned to the back yard his glass was full and Cassie had arranged the chairs so that they were facing one another.

He propped his acoustic on his knee and began tuning it. When the notes pleased his ears he looked at her. "What do you want to hear?"

She bit her bottom lip as she thought about what she wanted to hear him play. A smile turned up the corner of her mouth. "Do you still know *I'll be there for you*?"

He didn't answer. He just leaned back in his chair and started strumming. This was the first song he'd ever played for her. As he played he got lost in time, back to that first night. Their freshman year of high school.

Ryder had attended Jared's back to school pool party that summer. Ryder was the new kid on the block and was surprised when Jared showed up on his doorstep with the invite. There wasn't a ton of people there that night, just some of the neighborhood kids.

Cassie immediately caught his attention. Her pink polka dot bikini stood out from all the rest. She ran and jumped into the pool, splashing him in the process. When her head bobbed up to the surface he jumped in next to her, dragging her back under the water.

The two chatted while enjoying some water activities. Later that night a few of the kids were singing karaoke and Ryder decided to call his mom to bring his guitar. She did.

Instead of singing along to CDs and words on the screen, he decided to play a few of the popular rock songs on his guitar. The first one he played was *I'll Be There For You* and he looked right at her throughout the entire song.

Ryder was drawn out of his memories by the sound of Cassie's voice. He looked up to see her singing the words to her favorite song. Her voice was beautiful, slightly out of tune but beautiful none the less.

He played the last chord and her eyes fluttered open. She batted her eyes bashfully when she realized he was watching her, listening to her. She turned her head in embarrassment.

"Don't be embarrassed, it was beautiful." He put his guitar in its case and set it aside. Dragging his chair over next to hers, he gazed back up at the stars. "Do you ever wonder what might have been?"

Ryder's question was so out of the blue. Cassie just stared at him in shock, unsure of what to say.

"I have. Over the years something would remind me of you and I'd wonder what you were doing, if you were married. I wondered what would have happened between us if I'd stayed." He twirled a lock of her hair around his finger.

She was stunned speechless. Of all the things he could have said tonight, she would have never guessed it would have been that. "Yes, I have."

Chapter Fourteen

Cassie knocked on her boss's door. "Come in," he replied curtly.

She pushed open his door and poked her head in. "I emailed the completed document and all paperwork has been filed."

"Good. See you in the morning, bright and early." He never looked up, just typed away on his computer.

"Yes sir. I'll see you in the morning." She closed his door and waved to her co-workers. A couple of them stuck their tongues out at her playfully because she was leaving work a few hours early.

She had spent the last couple of days getting to know Ryder again. They spent their evenings chatting over dinner and stayed up until the early morning hours talking on the phone. Things were off to a pretty good start.

She could smell him as she rounded the corner to the lobby. Obsession lingered in every square inch of the room. She inhaled the wonderful scent.

The clacking of her heels drew his attention. He peered over the top of the magazine. A low whistle escaped his lips. "Looking good." He tossed the magazine on the end table and met her in the middle of the room.

"So where are we off to?" she asked as she gave him a hug.

"The carnival." He reached out for her hand.

"We're going to the carnival?" She hadn't been there in years. What an odd place for a date.

Cassie hadn't had that much fun in a long time. After getting over her fear of riding the roller coaster, she became addicted to anything seemingly dangerous. Roller coasters, tower drops, if it was high in the air and had the speed of superman then she rode it.

It took a lot of convincing to get her to sit down and eat. She looked up at him with her pouty lips stuck out. "But I'm having too much fun to sit down and eat that greasy stuff."

He chuckled at her. Here she was, a grown woman running around a theme park like an energized teenager. "I'm hungry, woman." He latched onto her hand and headed in the direction of food. "Corn dogs or that barbecued beef they're serving over there?" He pointed to a stand on their left.

"Corn dog, no wait, I want the barbecued beef." She tapped her chin with her fingernail. "Ah heck, I can't decide. Let's just have both."

He raised his eyebrow. "You're going to eat all of that food?"

"Yes." She tugged him toward the corn dog stand. "And a funnel cake."

"I'm surprised that someone as skinny as you could eat that much food," he teased.

"Shut up and buy my corn dog." It had been too long since she'd eaten carnival food.

He bought their corn dogs, a plate of barbecued beef to share, and a funnel cake. There was no way he'd be able to eat that much and he was a man. They sat at a picnic table. A young girl walking by with her parents shouted, "Hey, that's Ryder Hanson. Mom, we have to go back."

The mother shushed her child and looked over at the two of them apologetically. Ryder laughed. "Come on, grab your food." He gathered up their drinks and the plate of beef. "We better go before we have a crowd of screaming girls."

Cassie looked over her shoulder. Sure enough, several girls were looking in their direction. A large portion of them with their fingers pointed at them. A few squeals traveled across the way. "Oh my gawd, it's Ryder Hanson!" one girl shouted.

Another girl fanned herself and cried hysterically. "I love you," another one shouted as she ran towards them.

"Crap." He tossed their drinks into the nearest trashcan. "Run." He took off in a dead run, Cassie following close on his heels.

Luckily, a couple of police officers noticed the commotion and helped to ward off the screaming fans. Once they were outside of the gates Cassie bent over, completely out of breath. "Who knew that going to the carnival with you would turn into the workout of my life."

Ryder busted out laughing. She glared at him which only made him laugh harder. "Welcome to my life," he said after he composed himself. "Come on." He nodded toward the parking lot. "I'll take you somewhere else."

"I'll settle for a nice quiet place to eat my food."

His car was parked at the furthest end of the parking lot and Cassie thought her legs would fall off from exhaustion. By the time the Mercedes came into view she looked more like a walking zombie than a human.

Ryder drove them to the park next to the elementary school. They sat in the car and ate their cold carnival food. It definitely didn't taste the same cold but it was good nonetheless. Cassie leaned back and moaned in satisfied bliss. That deep fried food not only made her taste buds sing joyfully but it brought back childhood memories.

"I'm sorry our day of fun was cut short." He cocked his head when she giggled.

Instead of answering the question in his eyes, she wiped powdered sugar from the tip of his nose. Her eyes locked with his. So many emotions swirled around inside of her. Was it possible to still love him so deeply after everything they'd been through?

He slid his hand up her arm, to the back of her neck. He leaned forward, staring at her beautifully plump lips. Cassie watched as his tongue darted out, wetting his bottom lip. She wanted nothing more than to kiss him right now.

She needed to feel his lips on hers. To feel that connection that they once shared. She closed the gap between them and pressed her lips to his in a searing kiss.

His fingers tangled in her hair as he kissed her back. The slight tug on her hair sent shivers up and down her spine. Goose bumps rose on her arms. Her body melted into his and she wrapped her arms around his neck.

A thump on the windshield caused them to break apart. A basketball rolled off of the hood. A kid stood in front of the car, staring at them in disgust. He picked his ball up off the ground and ran back to the basketball court.

The two of them laughed. "Well, it's nice to know we can still gross out the kids," Ryder said as he gathered up their trash. He stuffed it into a plastic bag that he pulled out from under his seat.

"You keep bags in your car?"

He looked at her, feigning shock. "You think I'm going to spend this kind of cash on this car and not keep trash bags around?"

"You are such a dork."

"Maybe," he said, running his finger through his hair. "But I'm a sexy dork."

"Oh jeez, some things never change." She shook her head.

"We should do this again." He ran his fingertip along her arm. "Can I pick you up after work tomorrow?"

"I'd like that." Was she playing with fire? Most likely but at this point in the game she didn't care. If she only had a few weeks or even just a few days with him then she was going to make the most of that time.

"Great." He leaned across the seat and kissed her below the ear. "I'll take you out for dinner and a movie. Allie said there was some romantic comedy playing that you two have been dying to see."

"Yes, Safe Haven." Giving him a curious look, she asked, "You're actually going to go see a romantic comedy?"

"Um hum."

She felt his forehead with the back of her hand. "Who are you and what have you done with Ryder Hanson?"

Chapter Fifteen

As promised, Ryder showed up at Bradshaw Publishing to pick her up for their date. She crawled into his car and kissed him hello.

When they arrived at the Bijous she nearly choked on her own saliva. "We can't eat here." The Bijous was one of the finest restaurants in the area. There was no way she could allow him to spend that kind of money on her.

"Nonsense," he said shutting off the engine and getting out of the car. "I have a table reserved and I'm starving."

She watched him walk around the car and open her door, holding out his hand to help her out. There was no way he'd let her out of this dinner, this was where he wanted to eat and what she thought about the price didn't matter. The determination in his eyes wore her down and she accepted his hand.

This was her first time in a five-star restaurant. The expensive menu never did fit into her budget. Even now, she was having a hard time accepting this dinner.

They walked into the building, a young woman stood behind a podium looking at a computer screen. "Name?"

"Hanson, Ryder." He squeezed Cassie's hand in an attempt to quiet her fears about the expense. He had plenty of money and if he chose to spend it on her then he would. Case closed.

"Right this way," the young woman said. She led them to the back of the restaurant, to a private booth. "Your waiter will be out shortly."

"Thank you." He pulled out Cassie's chair, scooting her to the table once she sat. "I'm glad you decided to go out with me."

"Me too." A blush was spreading along her cheeks, she could feel the heat. Looking over the menu was a nightmare. She had no clue what any of the dishes consisted of. "What are you eating?"

"I haven't decided yet." He glanced over the top of his menu at her. Her big saucer eyes amused him. He knew perfectly well what he'd be eating but he wasn't telling.

A waiter dressed in a tux approached their table. Ryder ordered for the two of them without even consulting her. "We'll start with the French Cheese Platter and Bordeaux. Then we'll have a Filet Mignon and the Osso Bucco à la Bourguignonne."

The waiter nodded, turned on his heel and left. Cassie wasn't sure whether to be impressed or upset that he just ordered for her without asking what she wanted.

He smiled. "Don't worry. You'll like it."

♪ ♫ ♪ ♫ ♪

Dinner was surprisingly good. Cassie had heard of Filet Mignon but she'd never actually eaten it. She would have to figure out how to make it. It was nearly orgasmic to the taste buds.

The movie was spectacular, just like she knew it would be. Ryder even got into the whole romantic comedy. At one point she caught him wiping a tear from his eye. Of course, he claimed that he had an eyelash fall into his eye. She gave him an exaggerated eye roll.

Ryder pulled in behind Cassie's car. "Thank you," she said.

He looked at her, confused. "For what?"

"For tonight, dinner was fabulous and the movie was wonderful." She was thoroughly pleased with the night's events.

Ryder hopped out, meeting her at the front of his car. He hooked his fingers in her belt loops, tugging her close. "I had a wonderful time." He pressed his forehead to hers. If he could freeze time and stay in this moment for eternity, he would.

As he leaned on the hood of his car Cassie turned in his arms. It had been way too long since she'd felt this kind of peace, this feeling of belonging. She gazed up at the stars. Each clumped together to form a picture, to tell a story.

"You know," he rested his chin on her shoulder. "Tonight has been absolutely perfect. I don't want this night to end."

"Dance with me."

Ryder wasn't sure what to think of her demand. "Huh?" He looked around. "Dance to what exactly?"

She dug her cell phone out of her purse. Scrolling through the playlist, she settled on a slow song. "Dance with me." She spun around, holding her arms open in invitation.

Ryder didn't hesitate. He embraced her, rocking to the rhythm of the song. This night; the dinner, the movie, now the dancing, it was all so perfect. Cassie was perfect.

The stars shone down on them with their twinkling eyes. Crickets chirped their encouragement in the background.

A car full of teenagers drove by. One of the boys whistled at them. They laughed and continued their dancing until the song ended.

He walked her to the door, placing a large palm on the frame while she fished for her keys. "Cassie, I've been having a blast with you." He gently pinched her chin. She gazed into his eyes.

"Me too." She licked her lips, drawing his attention to their plumpness. "I'll cook you dinner tomorrow after work."

He dipped his head down to hers, kissing her. He broke the kiss but didn't remove his lips from hers. "Sounds good." He kissed her again then pulled away. "I'll see you then, Cass."

He watched her cross the threshold and then waved goodbye.

Chapter Sixteen

Cassie curled up on the couch with Ryder, leaning her head on his shoulder. He had shocked her earlier by offering to help her wash dishes. That was a nice surprise and she didn't refuse the help. They worked side by side, he washed and she rinsed. Something about it warmed her heart.

She gazed up into his eyes. So many times over the years she longed for the day she could stare into his dazzling hazel eyes again. Now, here he was in the flesh.

He reached over and took her hand in his. It was so much smaller than his, more delicate. Bringing their clasped hands to his mouth, he placed tiny kisses on each of her knuckles.

She sighed and closed her eyes. "I've missed this."

"Me too." That wasn't a lie. Cassie often occupied his mind while he toured the world. Missing her was most likely the reason that he sought female companions while on the road.

He rested his feet on the coffee table, content for the first time in ages. Music was his life, his passion, but nothing made him feel as complete as he did with Cassie in his arms. He inhaled the scent of her hair as he stared blankly at the television. Neither one of them was really interested in the movie but both pretended to be watching.

"Are you actually watching this?" he finally asked.

She shook her head. "No, I was just enjoying this moment." She looked up. His smoldering eyes lit a fire in the pit of her stomach. Glancing at his lips, she tilted her head.

This was playing with fire but she decided days ago that she'd gladly play with the scorching flames. Burn if she must. She needed to complete this bliss that she felt deep within. Her body craved his touch, his kiss, his body.

He leaned toward her, his lips so close yet so far away. He paused then leaned closer, their noses touching. Her heart beat so fast and hard she was afraid it might rip through her chest at any moment. The wait was driving her insane. Was he going to kiss her or what?

The feel of his breath across her lips triggered those butterflies in her belly. Now they fluttered around, her belly quivering delightfully. She watched as he licked his lips. The movement of his tongue gliding over his lower lip made her toes curl in anticipation.

He noted how her eyes followed his tongue, lingering on his moist lips. The spark in her eyes didn't just excite him physically. It reached in to his very core and keyed open a door that he didn't even know existed.

Years ago he knew he loved Cassie, he had never stopped, but this feeling that he felt at this very moment was beyond anything he had ever felt before. This love went deeper than he could have ever imagined.

Cassie couldn't take much more of this. If he didn't kiss her soon, she'd combust. She slid her hand up his chest, his neck, and into his hair. His silky strands falling between each finger. "Please, kiss me," she whispered.

He didn't move a muscle. The sound of her begging only kindled the fire within him. Her fingers twirled in his hair. It took everything he had not to give in and kiss her just then.

She ran her fingers through his hair again, grabbing a handful and giving a firm but gentle tug. "I said kiss me," she spoke with heated passion.

He licked his lips one more time before pressing them to hers. The touch of his lips elicited a moan from her. She melted into him, turning slightly for better access. Goose bumps broke out on her arms and shivers rippled across her belly. If this were a movie, fireworks would explode in the air around them.

Ryder's tongue darted out, demanding entrance. Without hesitation she opened for him, granting him access to what he sought. His tongue glided alongside hers, tangling and dancing about.

His hand held the back of her head, holding her in place.

Cassie sat up slowly, without breaking their kiss, and seductively crawled on top of his lap. Her slow rocking movements brought his free hand up to her waist. Sweat beaded on his upper lip and forehead. This was definitely the most intense kiss he had ever had.

Ryder was the first to pull away, surprising Cassie. Breathing heavily he said, "I can't believe I'm going to say this but," he paused, unsure how to word what he needed to say. "I think we should slow this down a bit."

Stunned, Cassie removed herself from his lap. He had been attempting to get her into his bed just the other night, was known as the womanizing rock star, and now he wanted to slow things down? Was it her? Now that he had her, he didn't want her? A horrific pain stabbed at her heart. She turned her head so he wouldn't see the humiliation and hurt on her face.

She placed her cool hands on her cheeks hoping to ease the burning redness. Tears sprang forth and she blew out a long breath to keep from crying. There was no way she was going to make an idiot out of herself. Not tonight and not with him.

If she so much as blinked, these darn tears would fall. She stood and left the room quietly. As soon as she was out of sight she wiped at her eyes, angry with herself for letting her heart lead her when she should have been listening to what her brain had been instructing her to do.

This was exactly the reaction Ryder wanted to avoid. What he should have done was stopped their kiss before it went that far. Heck, he wasn't one hundred percent sure that slowing things down was the best decision. It certainly wasn't what he wanted.

What he had wanted was to continue their kissing, eventually ending up in her bed. It had been there at the last minute when his brain took over and he ended their heated kiss. The reasoning behind this decision was not to push her away. No, it was actually to protect what they have going on in this budding relationship.

He stood. Should he go to her? He started to go but stopped. He took another step only to stop again. Running his hands through his hair, he wished he had one of those magic eight balls to answer all of his questions.

Just as he decided to throw caution to the wind and go to her, she stepped into the room. A saddened look on her face showed the pain his statement had caused. When her hormones had time to settle, she'd thank him for stopping their passion before they rushed into old habits. The only evidence that she'd even shed a tear was the small mascara streak by her left eye.

"Cass, I…" he began but was cut off by her holding up a hand.

"I'm really tired." She faked a yawn. "I think we should just say good night. I'll see you tomorrow. Okay?"

Chapter Seventeen

Ryder had plenty of time to kill before Cassie got off of work. He drove to the music store downtown. He needed new strings for his guitar. The building wasn't large but they had a nice selection of instruments.

He strolled to the guitar section and browsed for a bit. In the far corner he found a small boy, about seven or eight years old, admiring the acoustic guitars. "Hey there."

"Hi," the boy said barely glancing in his direction.

"Do you play?" He figured that he didn't own one judging by the way the kid was nearly drooling on himself admiring them.

"No, but someday I'm going to be a rock star." The excitement in the little boy reminded Ryder so much of himself when he was younger.

He smiled at the boy's enthusiasm. "I bet you'll make a great rock star."

This time the boy did look at Ryder, a smile spread from ear to ear. "You really think so?"

"Yeah, I do. You want to know why?" The boy nodded his head. "Because you remind me so much of myself when I was your age."

"Really?"

"Yes," Ryder answered, kneeling down to the boy's eye level.

"Wow, are you a rock star?" He looked Ryder over. "You look like a rock star." The boy was in awe of the man standing in front of him.

"Yes, I am." Ryder pulled out his cell phone, scrolled through his music player until his album appeared. He showed the boy the list of songs and pointed to the cover art above. "See that picture of this album?"

The boy leaned closer for a better look. "Yeah." He pointed to one of the four men on the photo. "Hey, that's you."

"That's right. I'm Ryder Hanson," he said with a wide smile.

The boy's excitement grew. This would be something he could tell his friends about. "Really?"

Ryder nodded. "What's your name?"

The boy stood straight. "I'm Lucas."

"Well Lucas, how about I show you a cord or two?" Ryder picked up an acoustic guitar, strummed the strings and crinkled his brows. "Hear that?" Lucas nodded. "It needs tuned in a bad way."

He plucked the strings, making adjustments as needed. When he was finished, he strummed the strings again. Much better. He sat the guitar on the boy's lap. "See these? Those are what you call a fret."

He helped Lucas with his fingers. "Now strum the strings with the other hand." Ryder helped him hold his fingers in place.

Lucas used his thumb like Ryder showed him and strummed the strings. "That was awesome."

"You, little man, just played a G chord." Ryder put the guitar back on the rack and looked around. In the corner was a Yamaha. He picked it up, tuned it, and strummed a few chords.

Lucas stared in awe of the man in front of him. "Wow, you're good."

Ryder laughed. "So, do you have a guitar at home?"

"No." The boy's shoulders fell. "Momma doesn't know how to play anything at all."

Ryder noticed the change in the boy's attitude. "Speaking of your momma, is she with you?"

"No, I'm with my grandpa. He had to pick up some groceries next door and let me come here." Lucas watched Ryder finger the strings, his eyes brightening.

"Do you come here often?" Ryder saw the fire in the boy's eyes every time he looked at the guitar.

Lucas nodded. "I like to look. Grandpa usually brings me here every weekend. One of these days I'm gonna buy one and learn to play." He pointed to the guitar in Ryder's hand.

"Follow me." Ryder walked the boy up to the front counter.

A second later, a graying man appeared. "Something I can do for you?"

Ryder placed the Yamaha on the counter and pointed to the boy. "I'm buying this for this young man here. We need a good hard case to go with it."

"Yes sir." The graying man disappeared for a moment, returning with a case.

Ryder paid the bill and handed the boy his new toy. "You take good care of this. You hear me?"

"Yes sir." Lucas beamed up at Ryder. "Thank you."

"You bet. Now go have a seat and wait for your grandpa." Ryder waved at the boy and left.

He had gotten so involved with Lucas that he forgot the reason he stopped there in the first place, new strings. Oh well, tomorrow was another day. He would stop by in the morning and get what he needed.

He crawled into his car and left to pick up something special for Cassie.

Chapter
Eighteen

Cassie opened the front door. Ryder stood on her porch with a silly grin on his face and a hand behind his back. "What do you have?"

"What makes you think I have something?" he asked with a flirty roll of his eyes. She reached for the hand hidden behind his back. He sidestepped.

"Come on, you know I hate this game." She crossed her arms over her chest. "Just hand it over." When he raised an eyebrow she said, "Please."

"That's better." He stepped closer and handed her a bouquet of flowers. "Hey there, beautiful." Then he kissed her lips softly.

"They're so pretty." She tugged on his arm, pulling him over the threshold then went to the kitchen for a vase. In the cabinet above the sink she found her purple tinted vase. She filled it with water and set the flowers carefully inside. It had been a long time since she'd had someone bring her flowers, not counting the other day. She set the vase on the countertop and admired it for a moment. "You thirsty?"

"Yeah," he answered from the other room.

She poured two glasses of iced tea dropping a slice of lemon into each glass. When she entered the living room Ryder was sitting on the sofa, thumbing through one of her novels. He saw her approach and closed the book.

She glanced at the cover and groaned internally. Heat rushed into her face. Ryder chuckled and she turned her head away. Could things possibly get any more embarrassing? She couldn't believe that he'd actually chuckle at her. Mortified, she handed him a glass and reached for the book.

"Someone's a naughty girl," he teased. He thumbed through the pages and then handed her the book, opened to a really steamy scene.

"You weren't supposed to see that." She glanced down at the page he had opened it to. She could feel the heat in her neck and face burning hotter, darkening the blush. "Just pretend that you didn't see that."

He chuckled, yet again, and drank his tea. "See what?"

"Good boy." She hid the book at the back of her bookshelf on the very top. She ignored the smirk on his face as she made her way to the sofa. The glass was starting to make her hands cold. She set it down on the coffee table. "I think it's time we talk."

"I agree." He turned so that he was facing her. She had grown more beautiful in her adult years. He kissed her lips, her nose, and her forehead. "I love you."

A tear escaped her eye, streaming down her cheek and dripping to the collar of her shirt. "You shouldn't say stuff like that."

A confused look crossed his eyes. "But it's the truth."

"It was also the truth years ago but that didn't stop you from leaving me." Now a steady stream of tears ran from both eyes. This was harder than she thought it would be but they needed to have this discussion.

He wiped at her tears and tilted her head so that he could look into her beautiful blue eyes. "I do love you."

"But don't say it. This is hard enough without the L word. I can't go through that kind of pain again." She wiped her runny nose on the inside collar of her shirt. "Allie told me about the call from your manager. They want you back next week to record the next album and plan the tour."

Now he was getting somewhere. All of her earlier weirdness was starting to make sense. "Yes, he did."

"So don't say that you love me." It was getting harder by the minute to talk. Her emotions were running out of control. "Last time," she sniffled, "you just left me."

"I had a chance to live out my dream, to sing. You can't fault me for that." Some days, even during his busiest tour seasons, he had regretted that decision. He didn't regret living out his dream, just not taking her with him.

She stood up and began pacing. She had to say it. He was going to leave any day now and he had to know. She had to tell him now before she lost her nerve. He deserved the truth. Pivoting on her heel she faced him. "I was pregnant," she whispered.

"I couldn't pass up…wait, what?" It was then that Ryder noticed the Yamaha sitting on a stand beside the entertainment center. Images flashed through his mind. Pieces of this crazy puzzle were slowly fitting together to create a picture.

"You left me and I was pregnant." She looked away, afraid that the pent up anger would resurface at any moment.

Ryder looked back at her. "Why in the world didn't you tell me?" It was taking everything he had to not scream at her, to not throw things against the wall.

"I tried." Cassie paced the space between the entertainment center and the coffee table, again. "If you remember, I called you over that day because I had something important to talk to you about."

"Tried?" he asked in disbelief. And there it was. The anger had finally broken free. "I don't recall ever hearing about a baby," he yelled.

She couldn't bear to face him now. She turned her back to him. "You came in so excited about your music deal. I tried to tell you that I had something important to say but you said you were leaving. You were going to record your first album and then plan your tour with the band that you'd be opening for." Every sentence rushed out of her in a shaky, barely audible, breath.

"That is no excuse." Now he was beyond angry, he was furious. There was no way he was taking the blame for this.

"You said 'I'm sorry Cass, I can't pass this up.' Then you just walked out the door. No goodbye, no farewell kiss, nothing. I got nothing. After everything we had gone through, all the love we shared, I got absolutely zilch." She finally gathered the strength to face him. "I never saw you again." She pointed a shaky finger at him. "You didn't even call after you left that day. Jared heard from you but me, the one you claimed to love, I didn't so much as get a letter."

What she was saying was the truth. He was guilty of being a jerk and leaving without a goodbye. And she was right; he never called or wrote to her. He was too afraid that he would either miss her so much that he'd give up his dream for her or that she'd tell him that she had moved on. His heart would not have been able to handle that.

On the other hand, she had plenty of options. She could have run after him that night, insistent that he listen to her. Or she could have stopped by his house the night before he left and told him. Another option would have been to tell his mother about the pregnancy so she could pass along the information. He would have been more than happy to take up his role as a father.

He pointed at the guitar. "So is Lucas mine?"

Shocked eyes looked back at him. "How did you know?"

He continued to point at the guitar. "The Yamaha. I bought it for a little boy I met at the music store today. Lucas."

Cassie gasped, she hadn't known that. Her father brought the guitar over earlier, said a friend bought it for the boy. She hadn't even seen Lucas yet. He had been on vacation with her parents in Florida visiting her brother. She didn't even know that they were back in Texas until this morning. "I…My dad brought it over a while ago."

He threw his hands up in the air, letting them fall back down to his sides, smacking his thighs. "Great Cass, real freaking great. That is my boy. Mine."

"I'm sorry." What more could she say?

"I want custody." His eyes blazed. "I deserve to raise my own kid."

"You can't take him from me." She fell to her knees. "He's my world. I'll die if you take him away."

His nostrils flared with each inhalation. "I really don't care at this point. He's mine and I fully intend to sue you for custody. You know that I have the money to make it happen."

Sobs racked her whole body. She reached out to him but he stepped away from her touch.

"If you're lucky, I'll let you see him in about eight years or so." He turned around and stormed out of the house, slamming the door behind him.

Cassie ran to the front door, throwing it open. Ryder crawled into his Mercedes, slamming the door shut. He saw her standing in the doorway. Hitting the steering wheel with the palms of his hands, he peeled out of the driveway.

She watched him until he turned the corner and was out of sight. She closed the door, leaned her back against the wood and slid down to the floor. Heartache and pain was once again her friend. There were no words to describe the way she felt. Excruciating pain didn't even come close.

Burying her face in her knees, she cried until her voice was hoarse and her throat was raw.

Chapter Nineteen

Ryder couldn't believe this. Cassie had known that she was pregnant with his child and failed to mention it to him. Didn't she know that he would have stayed? At the very least he would have found a way to record his music and still be home. Instead she had hid his son from him. Oh how that made his blood boil.

He looked at the tiny black box in his hand. Yeah, there was no way he was going to need that anymore. He tossed it into the back seat, not caring whether or not he ever saw it again.

The more he thought about it the angrier he became. Not only did she not tell him back then that she was pregnant but she hadn't told him since he'd come back either. That's the part that stung the most.

Ryder drove his car around town hoping to cool off. Unfortunately, he only grew angrier. It seemed that the more he drove, the more he thought about the betrayal, and the more his temper flared.

He arrived at Jared's house and found his friend standing in front of the window unit, shirtless. "I really need to think about some real air conditioning," Jared said, glancing over at Ryder as he entered the house. "This heat is for the birds."

"Yes, you do." Ryder stripped off his own shirt. "Where's Allie?"

"Cassie's." He sat in a chair. "Want to talk about it?"

Ryder took Jared's place in front of the window unit. "Why didn't any of you tell me about Lucas?"

Jared left the room to get two ice cold beers from the fridge. Handing one of them to Ryder, he sat back down. "It wasn't my place."

"Don't give me that crap. You've had eight years to tell me this." He drained the entire beer in two gulps, sucking in a much needed lungful of air afterward. He wiped his mouth with the back of his hand, letting out a loud manly belch.

Jared crossed his left foot over his knee. "True, but you still walked out on her without as much as a goodbye. You called me twice a month over the last eight years. How many times did you call Cassie?"

Ryder pointed the neck of his beer bottle at Jared. "That is not fair."

"Maybe that's how Cassie feels, that it's not fair. She is a single mother and believe me when I say it's been a tough road for her." Jared stood. "She never goes to the club on Friday nights. Do you know why? Because she'd rather be with her son. Her life consists of work, house work, and her son."

"I have no doubts that it has been tough raising a child all alone." Ryder was beginning to yell at his friend now, his anger to the point of molten lava. "But still, you should have said something to me. You're my friend, the one person I can count on and you sided with her to keep me from my own kid."

"Maybe if you'd had called her at least once," Jared started but was cut off before he could finish.

Ryder refrained from throwing the beer bottle at the wall. "You can all go to hell." He felt betrayed by everyone. Cassie should have told him but his friend should have acted as his friend and told him about the pregnancy when she didn't.

Jared was the one person he kept in contact with over the years and the idiot never once said anything about the boy. This was just great. Lies and betrayal by everyone. Then his mother's face floated through his thoughts. Did she know and not tell him? She had left town several months after he did. She had plenty of opportunity to learn of Cassie's pregnancy.

He had to get out of here. His temper was at a dangerous level and he needed to leave before someone got hurt. He tossed the bottle into the trashcan and left the house.

Chapter Twenty

Ryder once again crawled into his Mercedes. He needed to think things over. He backed out of the driveway. There was far too much activity floating around in his brain at the moment. He drove blindly, not because he couldn't see but his focus was on his son and the years he had lost.

Without realizing how he got there, Ryder pulled up in front of the building that all of his equipment was stored in. The building was just outside of the residential area at the edge of town.

He killed the engine. Behind those locked doors he would find comfort.

He flipped the switch and the room lit up. Making sure to lock the door behind him, he crossed the room to pick up his old friend. The guitar was a sight for sore eyes. He strummed the strings. Just a day without being used and she already needed tuning.

He plucked the strings, not aiming to play anything in particular. Time passed by and his plucking turned into strumming. Chords poured out of him with the release of his anger. Little by little words formed to the music.

"Silver blade across my vein. Cold, unrelenting, unforgiving." That is what Cassie's confession felt like tonight. "Simple task to turn the blade. Slice the flesh." Her betrayal couldn't have hurt worse if she had sliced his flesh with a sharp blade.

A tear escaped, slipped down his cheek to land on his arm. He stopped playing to wipe it away. The wet spot on his forearm would drive him crazy otherwise. As the music was silenced, Ryder heard a knock on the door.

He was pretty sure that Jared wouldn't come looking for him, his friend would be smart enough to know that he needed some time to cool off. So, who was at the door? No one else knew that he had bought this abandoned building to house his equipment.

Slowly, he walked to the door. Another round of knocking. Whoever it was, they weren't going away. He opened the door and was stunned to find Cassie's father standing on the other side.

Ryder raised an eyebrow. "Hello, Mr. Strong." He motioned for the older man to come inside.

"Hello, Ryder. I hope you don't mind the intrusion." Mr. Strong crossed the room and took a seat on the only stool in the place.

"That depends." Ryder leaned against the wall, arms crossed. "If you're here to plead on Cassie's behalf, please don't. I have no intentions on backing off. I want my son. Case closed."

"I understand that. I would be furious if I were in your shoes." Mr. Strong figured Ryder would be more apt to listen if he could connect with him on a father to father level. "I would absolutely pitch a fit if one of my children had been hidden from me."

"So you understand why I'm suing for custody then?" Ryder relaxed his shoulders when the older man nodded. "I didn't make this decision to hurt Cassie." At the sight of Mr. Strong's raised eyebrow he rephrased that statement. "Okay. Initially, I wanted Cassie to hurt as much as I was hurting but I just want to know my son. He is my son after all." He put emphasis on that last statement.

"Yes he is and you do deserve to know your boy." The two men stared at one another, not saying a word, for a couple of minutes. Mr. Strong could see the war taking place in Ryder's mind. The man was hurt, deeply. The young man also loved his daughter, Cassie, very much.

Ryder's emotions were playing tug of war. At one end of the rope, his emotions pulled for him to gain all rights and control over his son. To take his son away and let Cassie suffer the same loss he had. At the opposite end of this rope, his emotions struggled to pull him back to his senses. To forgive Cassie. To work on developing his family with her instead of trying to form it without her.

Mr. Strong looked down at the notebook he held in his hands. He ran his fingers over the dusty thing. It had been sitting in Cassie's old closet for years.

Ryder followed his gaze and noticed, for the first time, what the man held. He didn't say anything. He waited patiently for Cassie's father to speak.

"I dug this out of a box in Cassie's old room tonight. It's yours." He blew the remaining dust off and handed it to Ryder. "I know you think Cassie purposely kept you from your son. I don't deny that my daughter did the wrong thing. She should have told your mother and asked for a way to contact you."

Ryder couldn't agree more. "Exactly. I would have come back if I had known."

"What you have to understand is that Cassie also felt betrayed. She felt like what the two of you shared was nothing more than a high school fling. I'm not sure on the details of your goodbye but I do know that it stung my daughter's heart so deeply that she spent those first three months in her room crying. Allie couldn't even get her to go out except for doctor's appointments."

Ryder touched the edges of the notebook, flirting with the idea of opening it. "Three months of depression?" Dang, that was some severe depression. The anger in him slowly dissolved, turning into sadness.

Leaving his girlfriend behind to pursue his career was bad enough but knowing that she locked herself away from the world seriously made him want to puke. He hadn't realized the effect that his decision had had on her. He had been a fool. He had known that for quite some time now.

In the beginning, when his loneliness was almost unbearable, he tried to soothe the ache with alcohol and sex. It helped to take his mind off of Cassie but it never truly filled that void. He didn't understand why he felt so hollow all of those years until recently.

When he came home and saw Cassie for the first time, his love for her resurfaced. It had never disappeared, never faded. He had just ignored it to satisfy his longing to be a rock star. But that wasn't news to him, he'd come to this realization the other night. He knew deep down that she was the one, always had been.

"I think you should read that notebook." Mr. Strong stood. "You know where to find me if you need me." He clapped Ryder on the shoulder and left.

Ryder stared at the closed door for a moment. Curiosity gnawed away at him until he finally opened the worn out notebook.

The first page was titled *You Suck*. Below that, a picture had been taped to the page. It was a picture of him and Cassie the night before their high school graduation. He had snuck up behind her that night and snapped the photo as he kissed her cheek.

Below the photo was a short message. "Ryder, you suck donkey tail. I can't believe you'd choose singing over me. Why can't you have both? Oh and by the way, I'm pregnant."

He turned the page. "Ryder, you're a dang nincompoop. I sat across the street from your house and watched you pack up your things. I watched you drive away. You didn't call, you didn't even stop by the house to say goodbye." A broken heart was drawn under the message. "I hate you!"

The next page had an ultrasound photo attached. "Today was my first check-up. The baby is fine. He looks like a little bean. Well, I don't actually know if he is a boy. I won't know that info for a while." Another broken heart was drawn, this time with more squiggly lines to represent a shattered heart broken in two. "I don't really hate you anymore. I'm just numb."

Page after page was more of the same. A message about how great the baby was doing and how sad she was. Every few days she documented something, even if it was just one sentence to state how much she missed him or how bad it hurt that he'd left.

On the next page her attitude seemed to turn around. The page was titled, *It's a Boy!* Another ultrasound picture was attached. This time instead of a tiny spot on the photo there was a very visible boy part. His son was not ashamed to show off what the good Lord gave him. He smiled. "That's my boy."

Cassie's message was nothing like any of the others. "It's a boy. I just knew it would be. I hope he has your eyes and your talent for music. Your mom left town yesterday. I should have talked to her but I was too afraid that she'd hate me for keeping this secret. That or she'd think that I was lying about him being yours. He's perfect, just like you. I'm starting to feel him move, especially when I play *Come Back*. Yes, I own your very first CD."

She drew a line of tiny hearts across the page then continued her note. "I went to your concert tonight. It was your first official concert and there was no way I was going to miss it." She had been there? His first concert was in Utah which meant she had to fly just to see him open for the other band.

"You looked so good up there on stage. I'm so glad that you're fulfilling your dream. I wish I could have had the courage to go say hi afterwards." She drew a sad face. "But I was too chicken. Besides, I'm sure that you've forgotten all about me anyway. Oh, by the way…I love Come Back. Great job."

She had no idea, but when he wrote that song he was writing about her. In the beginning of his tour he missed her laugh, her touch, even her smell. It drove him insane. He continued reading.

"Every time I listen to that song I pretend that you're singing it to me, pleading with me to come back to you and make you whole. I know I'm foolish to hope for such things. I miss you. I will tell Lucas about you, about the man that I loved."

The notebook continued on with snippets of her pregnancy, the birth, and the life of Lucas. She listed his weight and length for every baby check-up, pictures of birthdays, everything until his second birthday. There were no more pages left in the notebook.

Ryder sat in shock. Even in her anger, her time of hurt, she took the time to capture the life of his son just for him. She didn't leave him out of their son's life, she documented everything.

The more he thought of this, the less angry he was. Besides, it wasn't her fault that he had left and never bothered to contact her. In reality, he brought this upon himself.

Chapter Twenty One

Ryder locked up his storage building. He gazed at the rising sun. He was tired after a long night of reading Cassie's journal but rest would have to wait. There was some apologizing he had to do first.

If Mr. Strong hadn't paid him a visit last night and shared with him Cassie's old notebook, he would have been boneheaded enough to sue for custody of Lucas. He had a bad habit of acting first and thinking later. And suing would have killed any chances of building a future with the woman that he loved.

He laid the notebook on the seat beside him, started the car, and headed to Cassie's. The early morning sun beamed across his windshield, casting beautiful colors on the dashboard. The birds flew in flocks over the small dirt road he traveled on.

The cows in the pasture on his left looked at him as if they knew what kind of idiot he had been the night before. They mocked him as though they knew that Cassie would never forgive him. His heart pounded in his chest. Was this the final straw? Could she forgive his bad temper and take him back? Well, he was about to find out.

It was still very early when he arrived at Cassie's. Not wanting to bother her, he stayed in the car and waited for her to rise. He practiced his apologies, all of them sounding ridiculous to his own ears. *I'm sorry* just wasn't enough. *I was a fool* didn't even come close to describing his idiocy.

Movement drew his attention to the front window. The curtains opened. Cassie stood there with a coffee cup in hand. The instant she spotted him parked in her driveway she turned away, closing the curtain with a swift movement.

He exited his car. There was a good chance that she wouldn't open the door for him but he continued toward her house in hopes that she would. He knocked on her front door. There was no answer. He knocked again. And again.

As he lifted his hand to knock for the fourth time the door opened, just a crack, revealing her shoulder and left ear. She didn't say a word, didn't even bother to look at him through the crack. A soft sniffling could be heard behind the door.

"Cass, can I come in? Please?" He heard her quiet footsteps as she moved away from the door. Pushing gently, the door opened with a little squeak. He strode in. A few feet away she stood with her back to him. "Turn around." It was a simple command. One that she was quick to obey. Her eyes were puffy and red from a long night of crying. "I've spent all night thinking."

Tears formed in her bloodshot eyes. "I really don't want to do this," she whispered. She had been up all night crying, worrying herself sick over the possibility of losing her son to this man. The man that she'd loved since high school.

He wasn't sure where to begin. He wanted to say the right thing. "I spoke with your dad last night." At the sight of Cassie's cringe he quickly explained. "He stopped by my storage building to bring me something."

Cassie gave him a confused look. What would her dad have that he'd need to give to Ryder? Unless it was her son. She fell to her knees, her tears flowing like a river. *God, please do not let this happen. I'll do anything you want. You want me in church? Done. Want me to pray? Done. Just please don't let Ryder take off with my only son.* She silently pleaded with God, hoping that he'd hear her and answer her prayers.

Ryder closed the distance between them, kneeling in front of her. "Hey," he whispered and cupped her face in his large hands. "He brought me your notebook."

She hiccuped. She thought she had that darned notebook packed away in her attic with all of the other ones. Every year she had documented their son's life. It was her way of sharing their life with him.

"I read every single page."

She buried her face in her hands. "Oh God, just shoot me now." That first notebook contained passages from some of her darkest days. Some of the content was downright hateful. In the beginning, her language was a little more colorful than it should have been. At that time, she wrote mean things to him as some weird way of payback.

"I'm glad that he did. That notebook has opened my eyes. I feel like a fool for the hurt I put you through. I'm sorry for leaving you to raise our child on your own." He leaned his head toward hers. "I love you."

More tears slipped down her cheeks. "What?" she asked in disbelief.

He tilted her chin with a finger, looking into her baby blues. "I. Love. You." He put emphasis on each word.

"But…" She looked at him in bewilderment. Just last night he wanted to sue for custody and this morning he comes waltzing in saying I love you? She shook her head, surly she misheard him.

His finger remained under her chin. "Forget about yesterday," he said just above a whisper. "I love you." He pressed his lips to hers. "I love you so much," he murmured against her mouth.

Cassie didn't dare move. If she did then this dream might end and she'd be transported back to that hellish nightmare she had been living in for the past few hours. Her tongue darted out to wet her dry lips.

At the brush of her tongue on his lips Ryder kissed her. She didn't kiss him back. Instead, she sat stiffly. He pulled back just far enough to lock eyes with her. "Cass, I want nothing more than to spend my life with you. I experienced a moment of insanity. I acted like a numskull and I'm truly sorry."

"It hurt Ryder. I didn't think my heart could shatter into such tiny pieces but it did." She bit the inside of her cheek to prevent a sob. The last thing she needed was for him to witness her blubbering foolishness.

He wrapped his arms around her, pulling her onto his lap. "If I could take it all back, I would."

She leaned her forehead on his shoulder, hiding her face in his shirt. "I thought I'd die from the heartache." No matter how hard she tried, she couldn't stop the silent sobs that erupted from deep within and shook her entire body.

Ryder tightened his hold on her, rubbing soothing circles on her back. There was nothing else he could do. He had screwed up. Again. The trust he was finally gaining over the past few weeks, gone in just a moment of stupidity.

With nothing else to do, he hummed. Her body shook violently as she wept. Why did love have to be so dang hard? In the movies it looks so easy, guy likes girl, guy courts girl, guy sweeps girl off her feet. Nowhere in the movies does it show this heart wrenching sadness where the couple is fighting to survive a brutal betrayal. At least he hadn't seen such a movie yet.

Her heartbroken cry ate at him, ripping a giant hole right through the center of his gut. If only he could go back in time. So much went wrong with their relationship. So much pain. It would take a lot of work but they could mend that broken fence.

Chapter Twenty Two

Cassie still couldn't believe the turn of events. Ryder forgave her for keeping their son from him. He was no longer suing for custody. Instead, he stood before her claiming his love for her and asking to be a permanent fixture in their lives.

She pinched her thigh just to be sure that she wasn't sleeping. Nope, she was definitely awake. Now she had one very important question to ask. "What about your music? How will you manage a family while you tour for years at a time?" She hated herself for asking but she had to know exactly where she stood.

Reaching for her hands, he pulled her to her feet. "I'll record locally." Her shocked expression put a smile on his face. Unable to hold back any longer he cupped her face, kissing her lips with tiny feathering kisses.

"What about the world tours?" she asked between his kisses.

"What about them?" He wrapped his arms around her waist, holding her tight. "I don't need any of that as long as I've got you."

She pulled back to look him in eyes. "Won't you miss it?"

"Maybe a little." He squeezed her tighter around the waist. "I can always perform locally and keep the tours in the states. If I can keep the touring to the USA then I can spread them out so that I'd be home more than I'd be on the road."

This was the best news Cassie had ever heard. Little butterflies danced in her belly. Ryder really did love her. He would not give up the world tours if he didn't truly love her. She smiled widely. "You would do that for me?"

"No," he said and her smile faded.

Her heart beat wildly with nervous anticipation. He wasn't cruel enough to say all of that just to say something stupid like "just kidding," was he?

The fear in her eyes stung his heart. Did she have no faith in him at all? That he'd come in here, proclaim his love for her only to spit in her face and walk away. If that's what she thought, he really couldn't blame her. He'd put her through hell. More than once.

She needed to be reassured of his love for her. She needed to know that his intentions were pure and his feelings for her were not fabricated or lust induced. "When I said no, what I meant was, I'm not doing this for you but I'm doing this for us."

"You're really going to stay?" He nodded in answer to her question. "Lucas will have a mom and a dad around?"

He smiled. "Yes, our boy will have a fully functional family."

Cassie squealed, joy overflowing her heart. "You don't know how many times I dreamed of this." Ryder lifted her off of her feet. "Pinch me."

"What?" he asked puzzled.

"Pinch me. I want to make sure that this isn't some dream." She flinched when he pinched the backside of her thigh, not because it was painful but because it startled her. "This is real, huh?"

"Yes, this is real."

Chapter Twenty Three

Ryder pulled his car into Cassie's driveway. The previous night the two decided that it was definitely time for Lucas to officially meet his father. That thought both excited and frightened Ryder.

He was nervous about meeting his son. Sure, he'd met him the other day in the music store but today he was meeting his son. Would the boy still think he was the best thing on earth after he learned that he was not just some rock star but his absentee father?

Cassie pulled in beside him. She got out of the car balancing a pizza box, her purse, and her briefcase. Shutting her car door was a challenge and she dropped her keys in the process.

Ryder ran to her side, picking her keys up off of the ground. "Here, let me help you with that," he said taking the pizza and briefcase off her hands. He glanced in the car. It was empty. "Where's Lucas?"

"He'll be here shortly. Daddy wanted to take him out for ice cream first."

Ryder laughed. "I bet that drives you crazy, him feeding your son…I mean, our son." It was taking some getting used to, referring to Lucas as their son. "I bet it drives you crazy that he's feeding our son ice cream before dinner."

"It does but today is a special day for him and quite honestly," she peeked over her shoulder at him, "I'm so nervous."

"Oh believe me, you're not alone. I've been sweating bullets all day." He held her door open and followed her to the kitchen.

♪ ♪ ♪ ♪ ♪

The front door opened and Lucas came in, tossing his bags onto the couch. Upon seeing Ryder standing in the kitchen he froze. "Mom." He looked around for his mother. "Momma, do you know we have a rock star standing in the kitchen?"

Cassie ran down the hallway, gathering Lucas up in her arms. "I missed you so much."

"Momma, you talked to me every day." He wormed his way out of her arms. "Do you know that a singer is in our house?" He pointed at Ryder. "Momma, he plays in a band."

"Yes, baby. I know who Ryder is." She took great joy out of the shocked expression on her son's face. "Actually, I want to introduce you."

Lucas shook his head. "I already know him. He plays guitar and sings. He's famous."

"Yes he is but that's not all. Come into the kitchen and have a seat at the table." She handed him a plate of pizza.

Lucas took a huge bit of cheese pizza, lifting his arm to wipe the grease away. Cassie cleared her throat and Lucas apologized. "Sorry mom." He took the napkin she offered and cleaned his mouth, forgetting about his messy arm.

Cassie took a seat beside her son. Ryder stood behind her, his hands resting on her shoulders. Lucas eyed his hands but said nothing. When he was finished with his dinner, Cassie took him by the hand. "Baby, I want to talk to you about your father."

Lucas beamed at his mother. "Will daddy finally get to come home?"

"Yes."

"So daddy doesn't have to work away anymore?" A look of pure joy radiated off of the boy.

"Not like before. Your daddy is coming home and he is so excited to meet you." She looked up at Ryder, taking his hand in hers. "Lucas, Ryder is your daddy."

"Awesome." He stood on the chair, arms stretched up in the air. "My daddy is famous."

Ryder laughed. This had gone much better than he had feared. All day he thought of ways this meeting could go wrong. Lucas could have hated him for picking music and fans over him and his mother.

Instead, the two of them watched as their son danced around the room singing about having a famous daddy. He stopped abruptly. "Does this mean that you'll teach me how to play my new guitar?"

"Absolutely," Ryder answered.

"Yippee." The boy jumped into his father's arms content and happy.

Chapter Twenty Four

It had been a long day at the office. Cassie desperately wanted to stay home with Ryder today and catch up on the sleep she didn't get last night. Unfortunately, her boss had called. She was needed ASAP to help train the new editor. Oh joy.

She tidied up her desk and packed up her briefcase. She was never so glad to see the end of the work day. Before exiting the building she said goodbye to Todd, the cover artist that worked for the publishing company. "I'll see you tomorrow."

"Bye, Cassie. See you later." Todd waved at her then turned his attention back to his computer screen. Todd was the first one at the office and the last to leave. With no wife or kids at home, he poured himself into his work.

"Try not to work too late. You're young, go out and live a little."

He faced her again, with a raised eyebrow. "Now you're starting to sound like my mother."

Smiling, she waved one last time and left.

The hot summer air stole her breath away the instant she stepped outside. It took her a couple of seconds to adjust to the scorching temperature. She walked around the building to the parking lot. Her car was parked toward the back of the building, at the very end of the lot.

Cassie stopped walking. Strange, there was a white van parked next to her. She looked back at the door she'd just exited. Todd was the only one still here and his car was at the other end of the lot. So, who could this van belong to?

She looked back at the van. It appeared to be vacant. Maybe it belonged to someone that worked in the building across the street. Or maybe it broke down and the owner left it there until they could have it towed.

Whatever the case, it wasn't bothering anyone. Hopefully it'd be gone by morning. She shrugged her shoulders and continued walking toward her car. She stopped again and looked around to make sure no one else was around.

The lot was empty, just her and the vehicles parked here. Again, she headed toward her car. She couldn't explain it but something wasn't right. Alarm bells went off in her head. Instead of listening to them and running for the safety of the office, she continued her journey.

Those warning bells in her head increased the closer she got. She ignored her common sense in her hurry to see Ryder and Lucas. She was glad that the two of them were getting along so well. She pressed the unlock button, opened the back door, and put her briefcase on the seat.

The sliding door on the van opened while she was occupied with finding her cell phone in the bottom of her purse. The noise startled her but before she could turn around a cloth was placed over her nose and mouth.

There was no time to fight this person off. The sweet odor in the moist cloth filled her nostrils, the chemical flowing throughout her body. A tingling sensation started in her limbs, her body was quickly shutting down.

No matter how hard she tried, she just couldn't turn her head back enough to get a good look at her attacker. Her body was becoming extremely heavy now. The darkness was calling out to her, beckoning her with a flick of its evil little finger.

Her eyes drifted closed and her body fell limp.

Chapter Twenty Five

Cassie woke up with a throbbing headache. She moved her arms so she could rub small circles on her temples to relieve some of the pain. One small problem, they felt heavy and she couldn't get them to move properly.

She blinked her eyes several times to adjust to the dark room. Nothing. The room was still pitch black, not even moonlight from the window shone through. She sat up and for the first time, noticed that she wasn't at home. Nor was she in bed. She felt the floor beneath her. Cold, hard, and mostly smooth. A concrete floor.

Was she in a basement, a warehouse, or somewhere else? If only she could see her surroundings then she'd know what type of building she was in. Or so she hoped she would.

Once again she tried to move her hands with no luck whatsoever. Though now her mind was becoming fully awake. This time she felt the tug on her wrists. Her hands were bound behind her back with rope.

She quickly discovered that her feet were also bound together and that stickiness on her mouth was a piece of tape. Great, she was tied up in only God knows where. This wasn't good, not good at all.

She pulled against her restraints but only managed to bruise her wrists. How in the world was she going to get out of this mess? She braced her hands flat on the floor and maneuvered herself backwards and over them so that they were now under her bent knees. Then she easily pulled each leg back, bringing her bound hands to the front of her person.

A noise outside the building drew her attention. A speeding car was headed in her direction. With any luck the driver would feel compelled to stop and have a look around. Then she could go home to Ryder and Lucas.

Tires squealed as the driver slammed on the brakes, bringing the car to a halt. Seconds later a car door slammed shut. Someone was here. Her prayers would be answered.

Gravel crunched with each footstep this person took. Cassie's heart pounded in her chest with her growing anxiety. Her accelerated breathing caused a ringing in her ears and she began to feel lightheaded.

Taking slow deep breaths, Cassie worked on slowing her heart rate. The last thing she needed was to pass out now that help was here.

A heavy door slammed shut, assumedly the front door. Stomping footsteps moved across the building, headed in her direction. The closer they got, the more she had to concentrate on her breathing.

The doorknob squeaked as it turned and a stream of light blinded her as the door opened. A switch was flipped and the overhead light burned her eyes causing a pain to shoot through her skull as it flooded the room with its brightness.

She slowly opened her eyes, blinking rapidly to adjust her vision. She looked at her surroundings. Cassie could clearly see that she was in someone's home, trapped inside of a bedroom. This was good. Now she knew that she was in a residential neighborhood.

In the doorway stood a beautiful woman dressed in an elegant evening gown. Her auburn curls fell loosely around her shoulders. If Cassie had to guess, she'd say the woman was about her own age. Twenty-seven years old.

The woman tapped her chin with a fingernail. Cocking her head from side to side, she looked Cassie over.

Cassie was relieved. Surely this woman would help her get the heck out of here. The woman smoothed the skirt of her dress before stepping into the room. Her smile seemed forced as she knelt down at Cassie's side.

Cassie felt a rush of relief as the tape was gently pulled from her mouth. She rubbed her lips with her bound hands. "Oh, thank goodness. Do you have a phone? I need to call home."

The woman giggled, which Cassie thought was odd. "Sure I do." She stood and left the room without another word. Cassie slumped forward. What did this mean for her? Was this woman leaving her here or was she going in search of a phone?

The seconds passed by like hours. Fear gripped her with its ice cold hands, squeezing every ounce of air out of her lungs. The walls around her started closing in. Fire burned within her veins threatening to take her very life.

Cassie's heart pounded in her ears. "Oh God, help me," she screamed as loud as she could.

"Well, I don't know about any god but I'm here." Cassie wasn't sure when the woman had returned but she was so glad to see her standing in the doorway holding a cell phone in her hand.

Cassie sucked in a much needed breath. The lack of oxygen had drained her face of all color. After several deep breaths her heart rate slowed and the color returned to her cheeks. Her eyes stung from the dryness. "I thought that you had left me here to rot in this hellhole."

"Don't be silly," was the reply.

Cassie relaxed somewhat. Now she could focus on getting that cell phone in her grasp so she could call Ryder and get the heck out of here. She held up her wrists. "Could you untie me, please? I'm sorry. I don't even know your name."

"Cheryl." She stood over Cassie with a sinister grin plastered on her face. "My name is Cheryl."

By this time Cassie was beginning to get the feeling that something was completely off about this Cheryl woman. "Would you untie me, Cheryl?"

A thunderous laugh escaped Cheryl's lips. "Why on earth would I do that?" She tossed her phone onto a chair that sat near the door before sitting next to Cassie on the floor. She looked her over speculatively. "Just what is it do you have that I don't?"

Where had that statement come from? Cassie didn't have a clue who this Cheryl woman was and the turn of events had her stomach twisting in knots. She was finally coming to the conclusion that Cheryl wasn't going to set her free. On the contrary, it looked like this woman was her captor. "What do you mean?"

"Come on," the woman leaned in, sniffing Cassie's hair, "you're pretty and all but let's face it. I'm prettier." She looked at Cassie's breasts. "I definitely beat you in the rack department." Cheryl cupped her own breasts, pushing them together. "I paid good money for this full rack of beauty."

Cassie's mouth dropped open in shock of what she'd just heard. On what planet did this psycho come from? Comparing her body to

Cassie's made zero sense. What was the common denominator? "Look, I just want to get home. I want to be with my family."

Cheryl's head snapped up, her blonde hair swaying with the movement. Her eyes met Cassie's and the hatred radiating from them caused Cassie to take in a breath. "You may have his son but you'll never have him. He's mine. Do you hear me, wench?"

"How do you know about my son?" Cassie was back to panicking now. The last thing she wanted was for this crazed witch to go after her son. "Who are you?"

"I'm Ryder's lover."

Chapter Twenty Six

Ryder looked at his watch again for what seemed like the millionth time. Where could she be? Cassie had called before leaving work to check in on Lucas. That was over three hours ago.

Something was not right here. She would never be this late getting home. If it was traffic holding her up then she would have called to let them know. He cracked his knuckles, something he did when he was nervous.

He pulled his cell from his pocket. No missed calls. No missed texts. He dialed Allie. It rang and went to voicemail. Odd, maybe the two of them were together. Those two were best friends after all.

He dialed Jared. It rang and went to voicemail. He redialed with the same results. Three tries later and Jared finally answered. "What man, I'm kind of busy here."

"Is Cassie over there?" Ryder paced back and forth. "She should have been home by now."

"No. I haven't seen her today."

"Maybe she's with Allie." Ryder was grasping at straws here. Freaky images of her being run over and left for dead were flooding his mind, scaring the living crap right out of him.

"Trust me, she's not with Allie. I would know if she was." So Cassie and Allie apparently were not together. Where in God's holy name could she be?

"Say bye, Ryder." Allie's breathy voice rang through the speaker. It sounded like Allie was with Jared, in bed. Not the image that Ryder wanted floating around in his head. Not now and definitely not ever.

Jared's ragged breathing came through the receiver and right into Ryder's ear. "I'll call you later." Ryder shivered at the image of what his friends could possibly be doing as he hung up the phone.

He stopped pacing and sat on the edge of the coffee table. More than three hours ago Cassie was leaving her office. She wasn't with Allie and her phone went straight to voicemail. He tapped his cell phone on his knee.

Where could that woman be? When he talked to her earlier in the day she sounded ecstatic about coming home. She was looking forward to spending a romantic evening with him. Surely she hadn't changed her mind and run away. If she had decided to run, she'd take Lucas with her. He sucked in a breath.

The more he thought on that the more he thought she had done just that. Maybe this was payback for running out on her eight years ago. Maybe she let him fall in love with her all over again just to break his heart the way he had hers back then.

He dashed into her bedroom. Throwing open her closet door, he checked to see if her clothes were missing. No, all of her clothes appeared to be there. Her drawers were all still full of her belongings as well. He ran across the hall to check their son's room. Nothing appeared to be missing there either.

He breathed a small sigh of relief. At least she hadn't packed their clothes and left the state. Or so he hoped. He pulled his cell phone out of his pocket and called Cassie's dad. Mr. Strong answered on the second ring. "The boy's fine. Enjoy one another would you."

Ryder gripped the doorframe until his knuckles turned white. "Lucas is there?" He held his breath as he awaited the answer.

"Yes," Tom said slightly befuddled. "I'm looking right at him."

"Is Cassie there?" He closed his eyes, silently praying that for some unknown reason Cassie was there.

"No. Why on earth would she be here? She is supposed to be there with you." Tom's tone rose with worry and anger. "What have you done this time?"

Ryder was offended that Tom would automatically assume he had done something to upset Cassie but refrained from speaking his mind on the matter. "Nothing. When I talked to her earlier she seemed happy. I had a nice dinner planned, Lucas is with you. It was supposed to be beautiful. But she never showed. Her phone just goes to voicemail."

"Have you called Allie?" Tom's voice wavered a bit. He was clearly on the verge of tears.

"Yes. She's home with Jared and neither one of them have seen or heard from Cass." Ryder had moved from panicked to outright terrified. She wouldn't run away without Lucas so what on earth really happened to her?

Tom let out a shaky breath. "Let me make some calls." He hung up before Ryder could say another word.

Chapter
Twenty
Seven

Cassie was terrified. This Cheryl person kept going on and on about how Ryder was *her* man. How many times they'd had sex, correction, how many times they'd made love. And every time she'd glance in her direction Cassie noticed the evil gleam in her eyes.

"Ryder? You're talking about Ryder Hanson?" Cassie swallowed, hard. Her eyes were burning behind the newly formed tears.

Cheryl stopped rambling and stared at Cassie like it was obvious who she spoke of. "Of course I mean Ryder Hanson. Who else would I be referring to, you brainless twit?" Cheryl cackled. "You didn't honestly believe that Ryder loved you, did you?"

Cassie pulled her knees up to her chest and hid her face behind them.

"You did." She snorted. "Oh, this is priceless." Like a hawk circling its prey, Cheryl walked circles around Cassie. "All that time he spent getting you to fall in love with him was just a ploy. It was me that he came home to. You were just a means of getting his son."

Cassie's heart shattered into a million pieces. She wanted to die. Words could not describe the amount of pain she was in just listening to this line of horse poop. If a Mack truck came cruising through and just happened to run her over she'd never feel it over her current state of torment.

The walls started closing in on her. The oxygen in the room burned up with every breath Cheryl took, every word she spoke. Darkness beckoned Cassie with a crook of its evil finger. She didn't want to resist. If she gave in to the darkness then maybe she would be relieved of the throbbing pain slicing through her heart.

She looked up at Cheryl. The crazed woman was still going on and on about her love life with Ryder. But soon her words faded into the background. Cassie smiled as much as her weakened body would allow. Any minute now she wouldn't have to see or hear this woman.

She closed her eyes as exhaustion took over and the darkness claimed her.

Ryder's phone buzzed noisily on the coffee table. He'd been staring at the darned phone for the last ten minutes just willing it to ring. Now that it was ringing he wasn't quite sure what to do. *Answer it dummy*, he thought to himself.

He picked up the device, looking at the caller ID. It was an 'Unknown Caller'. How strange. He slid the green answer button across the screen and put the phone to his ear. "Cassie?"

"Cassie?" Cheryl's voice boomed over the phone. "Why are you expecting a call from *her*?" Her high-pitched shriek grated on Ryder's nerves.

"Cheryl, we have gone over this several times." He was starting to get very upset with this woman. Could she not get it through her thick skull that he wanted nothing to do with her? "I have other things to do." And with that he hung up the phone.

He didn't have time for foolishness. The love of his life was missing. Walking across the room, he snatched his shoes up off the floor by the welcome mat and slipped them on his feet.

His phone buzzed again from this unknown caller, from Cheryl. He ignored the call. Again his phone buzzed. Several times in a row it buzzed. He rolled his eyes, tempted to just shut off the stinking device. If it wasn't for the fact that Cassie could call at any moment, he would have.

His car keys hung on a hook next to the front door. He grabbed them and locked up the house. The humid air clung to him like a jealous girlfriend, sweat instantly forming on his body. Well, so much for looking and smelling nice for his date.

He hopped in the car and sped away in search of his future wife.

Chapter Twenty Eight

Cassie was awakened by the sound of Cheryl screaming. She opened her eyes to see a chair being hurtled across the room. The lunatic cursed, stomping her feet like a two year old throwing a tantrum. She spun on her heel and left.

Cassie watched her exit the room, seconds later the heavy front door opened and slammed shut. She still didn't move for fear that Cheryl would come storming back in. Seconds ticked by hauntingly slow.

When the car engine revved Cassie exhaled the breath she'd been holding. Once she heard it peel out and speed away, she relaxed further. Now she could work on getting herself free.

She brought her hands up to her mouth, using her teeth to tug the rope free. To her dismay, the thick rope hurt her teeth and she had to stop before she broke a tooth. She inched to the door in awkward wormlike movements.

Cheryl had left the door open in her hurry. It was taking her entirely too long to get from the center of the room to the door. She feared that she wouldn't make it out before getting caught.

She was right. She heard the car as it turned the corner, pulling back into the drive. She cursed and tried her best to move back into the room before she was seen. If it hadn't been for these ropes, she could have.

Cheryl burst through the front door, lit cigarette in hand. She spotted Cassie on the edge of the doorway. "Well, look at you." She puffed on her cigarette.

"I'm sorry." Cassie prayed that her life would not be in danger for trying to escape. "I just wanted some fresh air."

The crazed woman chortled. "Fresh air?" Another puff of that putrid cigarette. "You know I wasn't born yesterday, right?"

"Yes." It was just above a whisper. Cassie suddenly felt claustrophobic, even in this open space. She watched Cheryl advance and flinched when she grabbed her chin in a stern grip.

Cheryl looked deeply into Cassie's eyes. She wanted to know why Ryder loved this silly little girl. He never fully gave his heart to her when they were on the road but she had hoped that his feelings would deepen and they'd live a long and happy life together.

This woman at her feet was nothing more than a soccer mom. And it made her want to spit in the twit's face. She always hated those types of moms. She hated them because they were everything that her own mother never was.

Her mother cared more about her drugs than she did for her. Cheryl had to raise herself. She was the outcast at school because her clothes were ratty and filthy. She puffed her cigarette then blew smoke in Cassie's face. "Ryder doesn't want some prissy miss-do-gooder. He wants a woman that can make him feel alive. Someone that can satisfy his sinful desires in bed." She looked down her nose at Cassie. "You, little miss, are not that woman."

She had no desire to sit here and listen to this woman talk about the many times she had sex with Ryder or how creative they were in bed.

Disgusting. Hearing these things hurt but this was not the time for crying. She needed to suck up her emotions, ignore Cheryl's lies and fabrications, and save herself.

She needed to devise a plan. Lucas needed her. She'd do everything in her power to escape this hellhole and get home to her baby.

Cheryl lifted her by the arms. "You'll have to hop your way back into the room because there is absolutely no way I am removing the rope from your ankles."

Cassie contemplated shoving this deranged lunatic into the doorframe and making a run, or in this case a hop, for it. Unfortunately, she wouldn't get very far and that would only stoke the fire burning within this woman.

She hopped back to her spot in the center of the room with the help of Cheryl. She had to change tactics if she was going to get back home to her boy. "Do you have any food in this place? I'm starving."

Cheryl had been quietly mumbling to herself, nothing intelligible just the ramblings of someone in need of psychiatric help. At Cassie's question she shut up, tapped her long red nails on her chin and thought for a moment. "I think I still have some oatmeal in the kitchen."

Cassie was not hungry. In fact, the thought of food made her nauseous. This was just a ploy, an attempt to break free.

If Cheryl brought her oatmeal, the only utensil she'd get would be a spoon. No, that wouldn't work at all. She needed something sharp, she needed a knife. What food could she request that would require a knife? "I was hoping for something with a little more sustenance, like a steak or something."

Cheryl doubled over laughing. "What? Do you think I run a restaurant here?" She stomped her foot, the sound echoing in the empty room. She no longer laughed. She just stared at Cassie with a menacing gleam in her eye.

"No, I know you're not running a restaurant." Cassie swallowed. This woman had fallen off her rocker. "I'm just hungry. I haven't eaten all day."

The woman eyed her suspiciously. She knew that the witch was up to something. If only she had the time to figure out what it was she was up to. On the other hand, if she were a betting woman, she'd bet that little miss perfect was one of those that prayed on occasion and went to church on Christmas.

She giggled. Maybe she should give in and serve her one last meal. Even Jesus had a last supper before his death, right? How poetic.

"Well, seeing how you're all tied up I guess I can run out and get you a steak. I'm getting a little hungry myself." She gathered her purse and keys. She stopped and fished around in her purse, pulling out a roll of duct tape. "I don't want you trying to call out for help." She slapped a piece of tape over Cassie's mouth.

This was not at all the evening she was hoping to have. This night had turned into one of her worst nightmares.

Chapter
Twenty
Nine

Cheryl stared at her cell phone in disbelief. The idiot was actually ignoring her. She had phoned Ryder several times and each time it rang once then was sent straight to voicemail.

Well, that didn't matter anyway. Cassie was not the one he needed, the one he truly craved. As soon as he realized what a fool he'd been then he'd come running back into her arms.

What her lover needed was a push in the right direction. She fished Cassie's cell phone from her purse and scrolled through the numbers until she found Ryder's. She pushed the text icon next to his name. *Ryder, I had to leave town. I can't handle another relationship with you. Tell dad to keep my son safe.* There, that should do the trick.

She turned the device off, tossed it into her purse, and walked into Roadies Steakhouse. The minute she opened the door the mouthwatering aroma hit her nose. The smell of steak as it cooked on the grill made her stomach rumble.

"You came in just in time," an older waitress informed her. "We are getting ready to shut down the grill." The waitress escorted her to a table near the bar. "What can I get you to drink?"

"Just water." What she wanted was a Screw Driver but she needed to keep a clear head. She couldn't afford to get buzzed, even if it was slight. Not when she had Cassie to tend to back at the house. "I want a Caesar Salad and a Rib-eye."

The waitress scribbled her order on a notepad. "Coming right up."

The delicious aromas from the grill drove her taste buds insane. She wanted nothing more than to order a big fat steak for herself. But as tempting as that was she had her figure to think about.

She had been living on rabbit food for years to maintain her sexy figure. If she started eating this fattening food and gained weight then Ryder would never want her. And she could not have that. If she had to starve herself to keep his attention, then so be it.

♪ ♫ ♪ ♫

Ryder pulled into the Bradshaw Publishing parking lot. He spotted Cassie's car right away. It was still parked towards the back. He called her cell phone again. No answer. Strange.

He pulled his Mercedes into the spot next to hers. As he got out he noticed that her back door was standing wide open. He looked around the parking lot then peered inside her car. On the backseat was her briefcase.

This was not like her at all. A knot formed in the center of his stomach. He retrieved his cell phone from his car and tried her again. Voicemail.

Then a text appeared from her. He read it but knew that what he read wasn't the truth. Her car was right in front of him, her laptop laying on the backseat unattended. She would never leave it out like that to be stolen. Something was terribly wrong, he could feel it.

The office had closed hours ago but there was another car parked out here. Maybe she was leaving and had to run inside for something, getting sidetracked. Deep down, he knew that she wasn't inside. He knew that this smelled of foul play but he had to check just to make sure. If nothing else, maybe the person in the building could help him locate her.

He rounded the corner. The inside of the building was dark except for a small cubicle in the far corner. He knocked on the glass door. No one answered.

He needed to speak to whoever was still in the building. He pounded on the door with his fist, desperate to find out what they knew about Cassie. He beat his fists harder and harder on the glass until he saw movement from that lit cubicle.

The guy approached the glass doors. "Sorry but we're closed." He turned to leave.

"Wait," Ryder shouted. The man stopped but didn't look at him. "I know you're closed but I'm looking for Cassie Strong."

This got the young man's attention. He went back to the doors, unlocked them and stepped partially outside. "Who are you?"

Ryder extended his hand. "I'm Ryder Hanson."

"Todd." He shook Ryder's hand. "She's talked about you."

A small smile pulled at the corner of Ryder's mouth. "Is she in there?"

Todd shook his head. She'd left the office hours ago. "No. She left at closing," he looked at his watch. "That's been over three hours ago."

"No, that can't be." Ryder pointed towards the parking lot. "Her car is still parked out here and her back door was standing wide open."

Todd stepped fully out of the building. He peeked around the corner, checking the parking lot. He looked back at Ryder, completely shocked and at a loss as to what this meant. "I haven't seen her." He waved toward the building, inviting Ryder inside. "I haven't seen her since she walked out this door."

"Is there a chance that she came back in and you just didn't hear her?" Ryder knew that he was grasping at straws here but he had to cover all of his bases.

Todd cocked his head to the side. The chances of Cassie coming back into the office without his knowledge were slim to none. "I've been in the back getting some cover art finished for one of my clients. I would have heard her come in but we can check just to be sure."

Both men went into the building calling Cassie's name. There was no response, just as they had expected. Ryder peeked into every office, break room, and even the bathrooms. She was nowhere to be found.

Todd met Ryder in the lobby. "I couldn't find her anywhere." A deep frown formed on his face. "I'm really sorry. Should I call the police or something?"

"I doubt they'd even consider her missing yet." He jotted down his cell phone number on a piece of paper and handed it to the man in front of him. "Call me if you see or hear from her."

"Sure. Please have her text me when you find her. Just so that I know she's okay."

"Will do." Ryder didn't even bother with a goodbye, he just ran out of the building to his car as fast as his feet could carry him.

Chapter Thirty

Ryder drove the streets praying for any sign of Cassie. She was nowhere to be found. He was past panic mode by now, he was downright petrified.

He jumped at the sound of his phone vibrating in the console. Snatching it up quickly, he answered the call. "Cass?"

"No son, I'm sorry." Tom sounded as deflated as Ryder felt.

"Any word? Please tell me you've had some luck." He held his breath, even crossed his fingers, as he waited for Tom's answer.

"None." Tom's voice wavered slightly in his fight against his raging emotions. "I'll see about calling in a favor at the Police station."

"I'll call immediately if I find her." Ryder ended the call and tossed his cell phone back into the console. Anger and fear threatened to suffocate him.

He slammed his fist on the steering wheel. Was God punishing him for his past mistakes? The steering wheel bounced under the second blow from his fist. He pulled over on the side of the road.

What he needed was some fresh air before he completely lost it. Maybe this is what Cassie went through when he left her to go on tour. This heart shattering ache that wanted nothing more than to chew him up and spit him out.

Making sure he had his phone in hand, he locked up the Mercedes and started walking the streets.

The waitress set a plastic bag down in front of Cheryl. "Here you go, Hun."

"Thanks." Cheryl handed her a tip, grabbed her bag of food, and left. First things first, she'd take Miss Do-Gooder her last meal. Then she'd set out to bring Ryder back home.

Cassie sat quietly, listening to the footsteps as they neared the bedroom. If all went as planned she might possibly be home by morning.

The clicking of high heels stopped abruptly. The bedroom door opened in one swift movement. Upon seeing Cassie in the same spot with the ropes still secure, Cheryl loosened her grip on the plastic bag and walked in.

The aroma of the steak hit Cassie's senses even before Cheryl took a step into the room. As a result her stomach rumbled painfully. She couldn't even remember when she had last eaten. She remembered eating a banana on the way to work this morning but nothing else.

Oh man was she hungry now that food was in the same room. If Cheryl didn't hurry up and give her that darned steak she may just eat her way out of these ropes to get to it. Oh, and she wouldn't stop there...if she had to, she'd eat Cheryl to get to that yumminess.

Cheryl sat down across from her, Indian style. "Don't move." When she was positive that Cassie would obey, she opened the plastic bag.

The food boxes were neatly stacked inside. She pulled them out, setting them next to her on the floor. She was tempted to eat Cassie's steak while the girl watched. But wisdom won out and she refused that hearty piece of meat knowing that it wouldn't do her body any good.

The more Cassie's stomach rumbled, the more Cheryl smiled. Jeez, the woman was getting a kick out of her torment. If only she could free herself, she'd slap that flippin' smile off of her face.

She waited patiently for Cheryl to untie her hands so she could eat but the woman never did. Cheryl just sat there with her salad in her lap, eating. Taking her time to savor each and every bite.

She closed her eyes and tried not to inhale. The pain in her stomach was enough to make a person pass out. *I swear child birth wasn't even this horrendous.* The world could be such a cruel place at times.

"You know," Cheryl said in-between bites, "I talked to Ryder while I was out getting dinner." Another bite. "He didn't even seem to know that you were missing. That or he just doesn't care. We made plans to get a beer later on." She glanced at Cassie to gauge her reaction and frowned when there was none.

Cassie struggled to maintain a straight face. She didn't want Cheryl to know just how much that statement affected her. Deep down she knew that Ryder was not this cruel person Cheryl was making him out to be. There was no way he could fake his feelings for her. The last couple of weeks had been pure bliss. But that didn't stop her overactive imagination from running wild.

If Cassie could just get her hands free she'd strangle the wench with her bare hands. This woman was nothing more than a thorn in her side. The sooner she plucked her out the sooner she could heal.

Cheryl chewed the last bite of her salad. She picked up the extra fork she'd brought in with her, handing it to Cassie. She slid the remaining box to her and stood to leave.

"Um," Cassie began, "I can't cut this meat with a fork."

Cheryl tapped the toe of her expensive heels, seemingly deep in thought. After a moment she shrugged her shoulders. "Well, since I have a hot date with Ryder." She made sure to draw out his name. "I suppose I can give you something to cut that with."

Cassie watched her walk out and sagged in relief. Her plan was falling into place nicely. Cheryl came back and handed her a butter knife. A butter knife? How on God's green planet was she supposed to cut through the ropes with a butter knife?

Cheryl smirked. "What? You didn't think I'd be dumb enough to give you a sharp one did you?"

"Of course not." She took the butter knife and began sawing on her steak.

"That should keep you busy until I get back," Cheryl sang as she left the room.

Cassie shuddered. She was so angry she could spit nails. The car started. She waited until the engine faded out before she began her escape.

Chapter Thirty One

Ryder had walked the streets for the last hour. There was no sign of Cassie. He'd received zero phone calls from her. It was like she'd just vanished from the planet.

Finally, his phone rang. "Hello?"

"Hey, baby," Cheryl cooed into the phone.

"Not now." He rolled his eyes. Could she just not take a hint? He was no longer interested in anything she had to offer. "I have other things to do right now."

"Where are you?"

"Look, I really need to go." He was in the process of hanging up when she spoke again. Her next words stopped him in his tracks.

"But I'm parked right behind your car. Where're you at, baby?" A bubble popped from her chewing gum.

"You're behind my car?"

"Um hum." More bubble gum smacking and bubble popping.

"You're in Texas?" He walked back towards his car, eyes looking in every direction. He was about four blocks away. If she was here, he wanted to know why.

"Yes, silly." She giggled. He hated the sound of her giggling. "Where are you? I want to take you out for a drink."

"Headed your way." He picked up his pace. "I'll see you in just a few short minutes."

Her excitement flowed out of her in her contented sigh. "I can't wait."

He disconnected the call and practically ran to his car. It took him a little bit to reach the street he'd parked his car on. At this moment he was glad that he kept in shape for the stage, otherwise he'd have been a real sight to see. He slowed to a brisk walk when his car came into view.

There she was, sitting on the hood of *his* car. What the heck? The creeper could have sat on her own cotton pickin' car. Nothing grated on his nerves faster than a woman who treated his belongings as her own.

Cheryl slid off of his car and sashayed to his side. There was a time when that would have excited him but now it did nothing at all for him.

"Hey there hot stuff." She stood on tip toes to kiss his lips.

When he stepped back she frowned. "How in the world did you manage to track me down?" This was very suspicious behavior. It was unnerving how stalker like this was.

"I missed you." She ran a fingernail along his jaw line. "I had to come see you, to be with you."

He grabbed her wrist, probably harder than necessary, and pulled her hand away. "I really don't have the time to do this. I'm out searching for someone that went missing earlier."

"Forget that witch. Cassie doesn't want you or she wouldn't have left," she blurted out. She bit her bottom lip. That was something she hadn't meant to say.

He froze, letting her words sink in. "What do you know about Cassie?"

Cheryl fidgeted. "Nothing, I...I just meant..." She twisted a lock of her hair around her finger. "I don't know anything about her."

He searched her face. The woman was hiding something. "You don't look like a woman that doesn't know anything. What is it?" The way she kept cracking her knuckles over and over didn't sit well with him.

"How about a drink?" she cooed into his ear.

Biting his inner cheek to keep from lashing out, he nodded. "Sure. Let's head over to the pancake house. It's just around the corner." He had a heck of a time prying her hands off of his arm. She clung to him tighter than a leech to fresh meat.

The café was nearly empty. The only occupants were a younger couple. Cheryl went straight to the jukebox. He ignored her beckoning and sat at the first booth he came to. She stuck her bottom lip out in a pout.

She made a big show by stomping to the booth, tossing her purse on the table, and sitting down with a loud humph. When he paid no attention to her tantrum, she began checking her emails on her phone.

The waitress came over and Ryder never looked at nor consulted Cheryl, he held up two fingers and said, "Two cups of coffee, please."

"Sure thing, sugar."

He breathed in a deep cleansing breath before turning his attention back to Cheryl. "So, when did you arrive in town?"

"Oh, um, just a day or so ago." She tapped her finger nails on the tabletop. She was nervous and tiny beads of sweat formed on her upper lip.

"Okay, Cheryl." He placed a hand over hers to quiet her annoying nail tapping. "It's time to be honest here. You are not acting like yourself. What in the world is up with you?"

"Nothing, I swear. I just wanted to see you."

"I've told you on numerous occasions that I do not want a relationship with you. So why are you here? Why'd you track me down tonight?"

"I…" She held her phone in a death grip. "I need to use the restroom." She fled the table faster than a criminal on the run.

Ryder pinched the bridge of his nose. This was not what he needed to deal with right now. Cheryl's drama was drawing his time and attention away from Cassie. He took his cell phone in hand and called Cassie, hoping that this time she'd answer.

A buzz from Cheryl's purse caught Ryder's attention. He eyed it, wondering whether or not he should dig in her purse and answer her phone. Deciding that it wasn't a good idea to go through the girl's purse, he left it alone. She'd discover it later.

Cassie's voicemail picked up on the third ring. Interesting. She'd turned on her phone since the last time he'd called it. He dialed again, hoping she was fine and would answer this time.

Just like earlier, a phone buzzed in Cheryl's purse. This time Ryder hung up. When he did, the buzzing stopped. He looked toward the restrooms. No sign of Cheryl. Opening her purse, he dug through the contents until he found what he was looking for. A bright pink phone.

This was the same model that Cassie owned. "What in the world?" He thought back, trying to remember what Cheryl had been holding. She'd had a black phone, much larger than this one and definitely more expensive.

Pressing the home button, he lit the screen. The wallpaper was that of their son, Lucas. No doubt about it. This phone belonged to Cassie. The question was; why did Cheryl have it in her possession?

Red flags shot up from every direction. This wasn't right, Cassie was in trouble and somehow Cheryl was involved. He had seen enough movies to know he shouldn't ask Cheryl about the phone. God only knows how unstable she may really be.

When he saw her emerging from the restroom, he slid the cell phone in his back pocket. Cheryl sauntered across the café. She smiled, manically, at Ryder as she sat in front of him.

"Where are you staying?" he asked.

"Oh, I just bought a house in one of the new additions going up."

Playing dumb was going to get old quick but the last thing he wanted was to jeopardize Cassie's safety. "I'd love to see it."

Her smile fell. That statement obviously didn't sit well with her. "It's not ready yet. It was just built and there's no paint or furniture." She avoided all eye contact. "We can check into a nice hotel though." She peeked up at him through her lashes, batting them seductively. "I miss you."

"I'd like to see the house first," he insisted.

She looked down at her phone, pretending to check her text messages. "I can't. Not tonight." Stuffing the phone in her purse, she stood. "That was my brother. He needs me. I'll call you tomorrow and show you then."

She left so abruptly that Ryder was afraid he wouldn't have time to pay the bill and leave a tip before she disappeared into the unknown. He stepped out of the café just as she was driving off. He hopped into his car, casually following behind her.

She spotted him right away and took him on a wild goose chase all over town. It didn't take long for him to realize that she would do anything to keep him at bay. He clenched his teeth. He hated being left in the dark but this situation was way out of his control.

He pulled over onto the side of the road. It was time to call someone with the right detective skills to handle this.

Chapter Thirty Two

Tom answered the phone on the first ring. "Have you heard from my daughter?"

"No." At Ryder's reply, Tom let out a sigh that was on the verge of a cry. Ryder held Cassie's phone securely in his hand and squeezed his eyes shut, then continued, "But I might have something for you."

"Thank God." There was a small pause. "What do you have for me, son?"

Ryder knew that Tom had some pull at the police department, he was a retired detective. "This girl that toured with me, well, she followed me here to Texas. I have no idea what she is up to but she has been pestering the crap out of me with phone calls."

"Spit it out, son." The rustling of papers could be heard over the phone as Tom sat down at his desk.

"She tracked me down tonight and mentioned Cassie, though I think that was an accident. Anyway, I agreed to a cup of coffee with her after that slip up. While we waited on the coffee she left to use the restroom. Her purse buzzed and I snooped. I found Cassie's phone in there."

Tom gasped. "Where are you? I'm on my way."

"Fifth and Ash." Ryder ended the call.

Cassie sawed at the ropes with the butter knife. It was a lot tougher than she thought it would be. She was working to free her feet first. At least if her feet were freed, she would be able to run.

She looked down at the progress she'd made. A small cut had been made to the top layer. Great, at this rate she would be here for a year trying to break free. Just her luck. She tossed the knife across the room in a fit of anger.

When she did, it hit something in the far corner. Cheryl's cigarette lighter. Hallelujah. She inched along the floor like a worm until she was within reach of the lighter. She picked it up and held her breath as she tested it to make sure it would light.

A bright flame shot up from the top and a huge smile formed on her face. "Finally." She held her feet as far apart as possible, stretching the rope.

Then she took a deep breath and placed the lighter under the rope, lighting it.

The rope caught fire and broke due to the amount of pressure from her spread feet. Once she was free she hopped up and began stomping on the fire. She almost didn't bother putting the fire out but then a thought suddenly struck her.

Cheryl could have had this house barred up and locked with double cylinder deadbolts. If that was the case, she'd burn up with the house.

It didn't take much to put it out. A few stomps of her foot and the flames were no more. When she was sure that the house wouldn't burn down she ran to the door. To her relief, it was unlocked.

She cautiously stepped into the hallway. Not a single light was on, just the light from the room she had just exited. Anxiety crept in and she fought hard not to panic.

The house was silent, almost eerily so. She prayed that no one was lurking around and tiptoed towards what she hoped was the front of the house. Each footstep echoed. She cringed. If this place was under surveillance, they definitely knew what she was up to.

When she reached the end of the hallway, she stopped. She waited a few seconds before rounding the corner. No one ordered her to stop. It appeared that she was alone. Hallelujah.

Moonlight shone through a small window on what appeared to be the front door. She raced to the large wooden door. The knob turned but the door didn't budge. It was dead bolted. She felt the lock. A double cylinder. "Crap." There was no way she could pick this, she wasn't talented in the lock picking department.

She was so busy thinking of an alternate plan of escape that she almost didn't hear the car as it pulled into the drive.

Cheryl slammed the car door. Ryder was a stupid fool. Why couldn't he see that Cassie was no good for him? That stinking winch needed to be dealt with once and for all. The sooner she killed her, the sooner Ryder would forget about her.

She marched up the steps to the front door. The moment she stepped foot in the house she knew something was wrong. The smell of burned rope lingered heavily in the air. Cursing, she flipped on the overhead light and removed her Taser from her purse.

She slid her heels off. Padding barefoot throughout the house, she kept the Taser up and ready. She eased around the corner to the bedroom she had left Cassie in. The little troublemaker had obviously found a way to free herself.

The room was empty. She glanced down at the food container. The steak remained untouched. "Brat," she whispered. A thud sounded in the direction of the kitchen. "Cassie, I know you're lurking around." She tiptoed out of the room. "Trust me, there is no way out. You're stuck here with me."

No response. That didn't surprise her. She hadn't expected the twit to give away her location by striking up a conversation.

As she neared the open kitchen she heard heavy breathing coming from the other side of the island. She picked up an empty coffee cup that was sitting on the table and threw it in the opposite direction of where she stood.

Just as she'd hoped, the noise startled Cassie and she crawled around the island. Right into the line of fire. Cheryl aimed the Taser at Cassie and pulled the trigger.

Cassie fell over in a convulsing fit. A huge smile spread on Cheryl's face. At last, she could rid the world of this disaster and move on to her happily ever after with the love of her life. She reached over the island, opened a drawer and took out the pistol she had hidden in the back.

She aimed the gun at Cassie. An evil laugh erupted from her as she prepared to squeeze the trigger. This plan was the best one she'd ever had. It was easier than taking candy from a baby.

Chapter Thirty Three

Cassie's eyes bugged out of her head as she glanced up into the barrel of the pistol. This was not how her life was supposed to end. She was supposed to see Lucas enter high school, see him off to prom, and eventually see him fall in love and get married.

She closed her eyes and did something she hadn't done in a very long time. Pray. Not a bargaining prayer but an all out, I can't do this on my own Lord type of prayer.

Cheryl's laughter echoed around her. Ignoring that hideous sound was next to impossible. The harder she tried to tune it out the louder it boomed in her ears, piercing her eardrums. Pictures of her life flashed before her eyes.

She relived memories from her first date with Ryder, the first time they made love, the birth of Lucas, and her reunion with Ryder. It was more intense than what the movies portrayed. Her entire life played like a movie in fast forward yet it felt like an eternity. With it came the emotions, so powerful and overwhelming.

As much as it pained her knowing that Lucas would grow up without his mother, she felt at peace knowing that he now had Ryder in his life. The two had hit it off perfectly. Lucas looked up to and loved Ryder very much. If she were to die now, she knew that her son was in good hands.

She opened her eyes, prepared to look death in the eyes. What she didn't expect to see was her father standing directly behind Cheryl, holding her in a chokehold. "Daddy?" Her voice sounded far away even to her own ears. Whether that was a result of the shock from the Taser or from lack of food, she didn't know.

Footsteps sounded in the front of the house. Seconds later Ryder materialized behind her father. "Oh thank God." He ran to her side, running his hands over her body in search of any injuries. "I was worried senseless." He took the pocketknife out of his front pocket and cut the ropes binding her hands. Then he lifted her off the floor, holding her to him tightly.

She was never so glad to see anyone in her life. His arms felt so good around her, though his hold on her got tighter by the minute. "If you hold me any tighter, I may not be able to breathe."

He shook his head. "Nuh uh. I may never let you go again." He set her feet on the floor and guided her outside while Tom did what he did best.

They stepped out onto the porch to a yard full of police cars. Several uniformed officers brushed past them on their way into the house. Two officers approached her with their notepads in hand.

Chapter Thirty Four

The trial was a nightmare. The press was everywhere trying to get their cover stories on the famous keyboardist gone crazy. Cassie missed several days of work due to the trial. Luckily, her boss understood. He even handed her a check and considered it a paid absence.

Cheryl was charged with kidnapping and attempted murder. The jury's verdict, guilty.

Now that the craziness was behind them, Cassie and Ryder could focus on the upcoming school year. Lucas was entering the second grade and couldn't wait to tell all of his friends that his father was a rock star.

Ryder's celebrity status was a huge concern for the both of them. Thankfully the school agreed to Ryder's demands of a guard on the premises for Lucas.

The weekend before the new school year Ryder was asked to sing at the local club. Cassie arranged for her parents to watch Lucas. Allie, Jared, and Cassie sat at a table as close to the stage as possible. All the tables lined the outer walls; the center floor was reserved for dancing.

Cassie was sipping on her coke when Ryder called her name from the stage. "This is a new song that I wrote the other day. Cassie Strong, I love you." He looked right at her as he sang. "Complete me, that's what you do. Make you feel like a woman is my specialty. Young and loving it, living for the day. Still be crazy for you when I'm gray, yeah! Our love is like fire. Burning hot, burning hot. Kiss me baby you're my desire. You're the one, you're the one. Won't stop burning, it can't be put out. Cause our love is like fire."

Her eyes welled up listening to him sing a song just for her in front of a crowd of people. This was exactly how she had always dreamed it would be. To have that sexy rock star sing to her from the stage, to call her out amongst the crowd.

Ryder beckoned her to join him on stage. What was he up to? Did he expect her to sing with him? That would never happen. She shook her head.

"Go on," Jared said with a silly grin on his face. With a push from her best friend, Allie, she hesitantly walked up on stage to join him.

Ryder took her by the hand and knelt down on his knee. In his hand he held a little black box. He opened it.

A shiny diamond stared back at her, an engagement ring. "Cassie, I love you more than life itself. I always have. I just went through a period of time where I was too selfish and stupid."

Cassie wiped at her eyes, her tears flowing down her cheeks in steady streams.

"I would be honored if you accepted this ring and made me the luckiest man alive by marrying me." He took the delicate ring from the box, waiting on her reply.

She nodded. "Yes, I will."

He slipped the ring on her finger, gathered her into his arms, and announced over the speakers, "She said, yes."

The crowd cheered them on. There were even a few shouts of "It's about dang time."

Chapter Thirty Five

The wedding had a large turnout. The press was kept at bay thanks to the police department. Lucas was ecstatic about being the best man. He stood proud and tall next to Ryder at the ceremony.

The honeymoon was a short weekend getaway to Hawaii with Lucas in tow. Not exactly the romantic getaway they'd hoped for but they couldn't resist taking their son along after he discovered where they were going.

Cassie stretched out on her towel, watching her favorite boys swim in the pool. Ryder resurfaced and caught her staring. He smiled. "Come in," he shouted.

"No thanks. I'm fine right here, reading this fabulous book." She held the book up in the air. "And I'm working on my tan."

He said something to one of his body guards. Cassie strained to hear but he spoke so low that his voice didn't travel to her ears. By the look on his face, he was up to something. His mischievous eyes met hers and her stomach quivered.

He exited the pool and walked toward her, shaking water off his body with every stride. He scooped her up in his arms and continued his fast paced walk to their hotel room.

"What are you doing?" she asked, looking back at her son.

"Lucas is fine. He has the guards to look over him." He gave her backside a playful slap. "You are going to join me in our room. We're here for our honeymoon and we've done very little honeymooning."

She giggled. "I love you."

He kicked the door shut behind him. "I love you too." He laid her on the king-size bed, pulling her bikini bottoms off in the process. He watched her, eyes blazing, as he pulled his swimming shorts off.

She untied her top as he climbed on the bed next to her, hovering over her. He kissed her tenderly, biting her bottom lip. That nip sent shivers all the way to her toes. She arched her back. Running her hands over his shoulders and down his thick muscular back she let out a moan.

He settled between her legs and eased himself into her. Being with Cassie again, united body and soul, was heaven on earth.

Lyrics

The song in Ryder's darker moment

Temptation written by Andrea L. Staum

refrain - Do you know your demons?
They should be your friends
Learn them, respect them, fear them

Silver blade across my vein
Cold, unrelenting, unforgiving
Simple task to turn the blade
-Slice the flesh
Resist temptation and know my limits

refrain

Lustful thoughts cross my mind
Hot, unbidden, unforgiving
Simple task to find someone for the night
Resist temptation and know my limits

refrain

Blood red rage blinding me
Encompassing, unyielding, unforgiving
Simple task to find a fight and release
Resist temptation and know your limits

Come Back (the song from chapter one & Cassie's notebook)

Come Back written by Ti Colluney

The silence in my head is too loud
Panic hits but it's too late
Too late to say what you needed to hear
You needed to hear
Just how much I need you
And now you took the better part of me

Come back, Come back
Come back and make me whole
Come back, Come back
Come back and see me live

Silly words mean so much
I should have said them more
Never should have let you go
My eyes are now open
Open wide to see
Just how much you complete me
And now I am lost
And the silence in my head is loud

Too loud
So loud

Come back, Come back
Come back and make me whole
Come back, Come back
Come back and we both can smile again

Come back to me and bring me my light
Come back and let me breathe again
I need your warmth, your love, your soul
Because without you
I am lost

Come back, Come back
I want to be whole again
Come back, Come back
Bring back the light to my world again
Come back, Come back
Come
Back

Our Love is like Fire

Our Love is like Fire written by Tom Brewster

I wasn't looking for love but I found you
anyway
You didn't know that I was the man who
would steal your heart away
We're like peas in a pod, fire and gasoline
We can't be put out, won't stop loving,
yeah!

Complete me, that's what you do
Make you feel like a woman is my specialty
Young and loving it, living for the day
Still be crazy for you when I'm gray, yeah!

Our love is like fire
Burning hot, burning hot
Kiss me baby you're my desire
You're the one, you're the one
Won't stop burning, it can't be put out
Cause our love is like fire

Our love is getting hotter
Smoking white hot
Can't contain this feeling
It's never gonna stop, never gonna stop, no

it will never stop

Our love is like fire
Burning hot, burning hot
Kiss me baby you're my desire
You're the one, you're the one
Won't stop burning, it can't be put out
Cause our love is like fire

Other books by Tich Brewster…

Young Adult:

Angels & Demons series…
Devada
Divulgence

New Adult:

Royal Blood series…
Princesses of the Night
Hold Fast
Betrayal

ABOUT THE AUTHOR

Tich is an Oklahoma resident and the mother of five. Her passion for reading started at an early age when her Aunt Vicky gave her the novel Heidi for Christmas. She didn't start writing until middle school, after being inspired by her best friend's short stories. "Genny's stories weren't just great but they inspired me to put my pen and paper to good use." Tich never thought of publishing her works until working with Teresa Fuentez on the Royal Blood series.

Find her on the web at www.tichbrewster.com

www.ingramcontent.com/pod-product-compliance
Lightning Source LLC
Chambersburg PA
CBHW051413170626
46809CB00006B/2142